A Tiger's Bride

(A Lion's Pride, #4)

By
Eve Langlais

Copyright and Disclaimer

Copyright © April 2015, Eve Langlais
Cover Art by Yocla Designs © July 2015
Edited by Devin Govaere
Copy Edited by Amanda L. Pederick
Produced in Canada

Published by Eve Langlais
1606 Main Street, PO Box 151
Stittsville, Ontario, Canada, K2S1A3
http://www.EveLanglais.com

ISBN-13: 978-1515097495
ISBN-10: 1515097498

Chapter One

How much trouble would it cause if I kidnapped the bride before the wedding took place?

Probably more than Meena was worth—despite her formidable genes—and that was why Dmitri sat in a chair in the back row of the temporary outdoor reception area instead of plotting a grand abduction.

And, no, his disgruntled mien did not mean he sulked. He pitied Meena for making the wrong choice. Clearly, he would have made the much better husband. Fact, not arrogance, made him so sure.

Alas, Meena didn't grasp his greatness. She'd rejected his proposal of marriage—to his shock—not that he'd taken no for an answer. As soon as he'd laid eyes on her splendid hips—made for bearing big, strong cubs—he'd wanted her to start his dynasty of tigons.

He should clarify, he didn't mean Tiggers, which his sister purposely teased when she heard of his plan. Tigons were his goal, a tiger/lion mix, a formidable blend that resulted in strength, size, and a fabulous fur. However, to create this wonderful hybrid mix, he needed the perfect mate. As a male Siberian tiger in splendid health, with excellent lineage, physical stature, and lush hair, he already possessed great size. Add his excellent genes to that of a robust lioness and he'd make super babies.

Or he would have if some other man hadn't stolen Meena from him. Never mind the fact that

Meena was less than enamored with his plan, to the point that she escaped him—the locked door, bars on the windows, and remote location not proving a hindrance—before he could get a ring on her finger. Sure, he'd noticed her reluctance. However, she would have eventually come around. Who wouldn't love him? His mother declared him perfect. His grandmother said he did their lineage proud. As for his sister? Who cared what she said?

But no, Meena had to prove stubborn and end up rejecting him in favor of an omega liger. The shame. The disappointment. The relief that he wouldn't have to deal with the stubborn female.

In a sense, Meena had done him a favor. The more he found himself subjected to her antics, the more he realized they simply wouldn't have suited. At all.

For one, Dmitri preferred his women docile. He had enough controlling women in his life starting with his mother—*"You are not wearing that, are you? Here, let me choose something more appropriate. We do have an image to maintain, after all, with the lower classes."* Czarina indeed. His mother suffered under delusions of grandeur and a past where their family reigned.

Then there was his sister and grandmother, both of them with way too many opinions on a suitable wife for a Russian lord—a mob lord, but still someone of importance. While the populace at large, at least the human one, might not recognize his superiority and dominance, those in the shifter world in Mother Russia recognized him for what and who he was. A powerful man that no one should ever screw with.

Meena dared to screw with him. Defied him. Escaped him and, in minutes, would become another male's problem. Surely his inner feline didn't breathe a sigh of relief?

As for him, he was back to square one. No wife. No prospect. No—

Something yummy comes our way.

Indeed something delicious did come sauntering past with wide hips, towering legs, and a scent that made him want to roll on his back and thrust his legs in the air so he could enjoy a good wiggle. He practically drooled at the gorgeous womanly shape that caught his eye. And as for her face? She looked just like Meena yet wasn't her.

What's this? Did the genetically perfect Meena have a sister? An unmarried one? Could he be so lucky?

A murmur went through the crowd, and he caught the phrase, repeated more than once by a few people present, "Here comes trouble."

Surely they didn't speak of the goddess he currently undressed with his eyes.

Riveted, he couldn't help but stare at the statuesque blonde as she walked the aisle with grace, head held high, long neck tempting, hips swishing. The picture of elegance. At least she was until her heel caught on a wrinkle in the red carpet and she squeaked as she went flying.

Almost, he went soaring from his seat to save her, but too many hands were already aiding her in regaining her footing. To dash to her rescue now would bring too much undue attention.

We must hide our interest lest people take note.

However, keeping his intrigue secret might prove hard, given he couldn't take his eyes from the woman. She called to him.

Want her. It wasn't just his tiger that felt an urge to rub against the delightful creature.

The gears in his mind turned as he plotted.

Perhaps this trip to America would not be wasted after all.

Moments later, when his ex-fiancée strode past on her father's arm, he paid no attention. Who cared? Certainly not him. Funny how Meena in her white gown didn't draw a single glance from him, and yet he'd memorized every inch of the unknown woman. The resemblance to his former fiancée was startling, and yet, at the same time, he noted the distinct differences. For one, the way they carried themselves. The object of his interest somehow managed a fragile appearance that belied her incredible stature.

The ceremony no sooner finished than Dmitri was on the prowl, moving with steady purpose toward his future bride—he ever was a man of snap decisions—until a burly man stepped in his way.

Not a small man himself, Dmitri didn't balk in the face of the man's glare. On the contrary, head held at an imperious angle—taught to him at a young age by his mother who insisted lords should always look down at the world, even if the world was taller—Dmitri arched a brow and, with an arrogance only the great can achieve, said, "You are in my way." The unspoken remainder of his sentence was, *move before I move you.*

Except, apparently, the rather large fellow didn't grasp intimidation, probably because he projected a good dose of it himself. Meena's father wasn't one to bow before anyone despite his blue-collar status. "What the hell are you doing eying my daughter?"

"Is it not the prerogative of a jilted fiancé to lament the loss of a stupendous woman?"

Peter, whom he'd met the night before over vodka and arm wrestling, snorted. "Oh please, we both know you weren't in love with my Meena."

"I planned to marry her."

"To make super babies. I know. We all know. And you lost her. But you know I was talking about my other daughter. Teena. You were eyeballing her as if she were a fresh-cut piece of porterhouse steak begging to get eaten. And I'm telling you right now to stop it."

Teena. He had a name. He also had a threat to deal with. The day was getting brighter by the moment. "Your daughter, Teena, is she single?"

A low growl rumbled from Peter. "Doesn't matter if she is or not. You stay away from her. She's not like her sister. She's fragile."

And clumsy, given she managed to whirl and knock a waiter with a tray of drinks on his ass. At least the glasses that spilled held white wine, which meant only wet spots and not stains on those who received a dousing.

"What makes you think I would treat her with less than utmost courtesy?"

"I can see your devious mind churning. You didn't get one daughter, so now you're aiming to go after the other. Listen, boy, I don't know how it works in Russia, but here in the good ol' U S of A, we don't stalk women and force them to get married. Whether we like it or not, there's something called women's lib which means they get a choice in who they spend their lives with."

"So if I give her a choice, then you would accept my suit?"

"No."

"Why not? I am wealthy. Well bred. I assure you, I am not one to philander. I would take my vow very seriously. So again, I ask, why not?"

That question caused drawn brows. "Don't fuck with me, boy. And don't fuck with my daughter.

Teena's too innocent to deal with a fellow like you."

Innocent? What a lovely tidbit. His determination to possess her only grew, despite her father's objections. "I think the choice should belong to your daughter."

"And I'm telling you right now I won't stand for you stalking Teena like you did Meena."

Dmitri pursed his lips and made a noise. "The term stalking is rather harsh, don't you think? Your daughter agreed to our engagement. It is not my fault she later got cold feet."

Peter rolled his eyes. "Are all Russians this arrogant and stupid? She never agreed. You locked her up. Now listen, you mule-headed moron, because I won't warn you again. Stay. Away. From. Teena. The only reason you're still alive is because I promised the pride's alpha to not start a diplomatic nightmare. But give me enough reason and you and I will be making a visit to the woods. If we do, only one of us will be leaving it alive."

Not one to cower before threats, Dmitri stretched his lips in what his enemies labeled his scary smile. "Anytime you want to visit the woods, let me know, although you might want to make your goodbyes before we do. I'm sure your family will probably miss you." Confidence, Dmitri's best friend since childhood.

His reply surprised the older man, who barked out a laugh. "By damn, you've got balls, boy. I'll give you that, and under other circumstance, perhaps I might have let you court my baby girl. However, no way am I allowing my delicate kitten to marry some foreigner and move overseas."

Dmitri took those words as a partial acceptance of his suit, a suit he didn't repeat aloud. No need to warn those opposed about his plans.

And he did have plans, seductive ones, nefarious ones. Whatever a person wanted to call them, he didn't intend to leave this party unless a certain lady was with him.

Willing or not.

Rawr.

Chapter Two

The stare between her shoulder blades burned. Tingled. It roused her curious cat. It made Teena want to turn around and peek. Yet, she knew it would look odd if she did. She was, after all, on display as maid of honor.

Still, though, she really wanted to know who the hell watched her so intently.

She'd felt the weight of the stare almost the instant she walked down the aisle. Even odder, the awareness someone watched her avidly didn't frighten her. On the contrary, it roused awareness, a molten warmth that fired through her veins awakening all her senses.

This hyper awareness was what she blamed on her somewhat less-than-graceful trip—that and the muttered, but clearly understood, "Here comes trouble."

They were quite right in their assessment. Teena certainly proved over and over again that she was a magnet for it, especially when in the spotlight, like now.

The red carpet, placed atop manicured lawn, held one tiny wrinkle and, along with her high heel shoes, conspired against her.

If a lioness falls at the wedding, everyone hears—and comments.

"Oooh," uttered from a watching crowd. Crunch as she hit. Then the panicky wail of her aunt,

"Someone pull her off, she's crushing poor Uncle George."

He wasn't the only one who broke her fall.

Whee, look at me, I managed to take out three wedding guests at once.

Cheeks hot—a habit she hadn't managed to shake over the years, despite her numerous mishaps—she'd regained her feet with some helping hands. However, forget taking a step in her heels. One wobbled precariously, thus, with a red face surely rivaling that of a ripe tomato, she slipped off her heels and, with them dangling from her fingers, finished her less-than-noble walk down the carpeted aisle.

As she stood at the head of the attending guests, in her place as maid of honor, she had a chance to scan the crowd. It took only a moment to discover the culprit behind the stare. It belonged to a man in the very back, dressed elegantly in a dark gray suit that fitted his wide shoulders to perfection. His long legs were stretched to the side, his feet dangling in the aisle. A tall man. A sensuously sexy male with black hair, touched with a hint of red-gold, and eyes that riveted her in place.

Her tummy fluttered, and the heat flooding her cheeks this time had nothing to do with embarrassment.

We are admired. Her inner lioness preened before the evident visual praise.

Teena wanted to cringe. Wouldn't it figure that this most handsome of men would see her stumble? Then again, was she really surprised? Her track record with men wasn't very good, and her propensity for trouble didn't help. For a girl who believed in happily ever afters, she seemed to encounter a lot of zeros instead of heroes.

But hey, if Meena can find a man, so can I.

Her twin sister, with her bold nature and less-than-ladylike ways, had been voted in high school most likely to get stranded on a desert island or killed by one of her victims.

Yet Meena had found her mate, and a handsome one, too, who, in a romantic twist, planned the surprise wedding Teena currently attended. A surprise wedding that included one jilted fiancé.

Given she didn't recognize the stranger, and his aristocratic bearing seemed out of place, it struck Teena in that instance who the man must be. No wonder he eyed her with such interest.

So this is the infamous Dmitri.

He's hot. And he's eyeballing me.

It didn't take a genius, once she connected the dots, to understand where his interest came from. He couldn't get one sister, so now he would set his sights on the other.

A pity she hadn't met him first. Teena would have loved to have been the ardent object of this man's attention, even if his reasoning—which Meena screeched at length was centered around birthing hips—was less than sound.

In the beginning, perhaps the hot Russian male would have wanted her for her genes, but in the end, Teena would have made him love her. Or accidentally killed him in the attempt.

When the ceremony ended, Teena noted, with held breath, that he made a beeline toward her, a straight path interrupted by one very overprotective father.

Sigh.

There went any fantasy of this Dmitri fellow sweeping her off her feet and working to convince her to accept him as her man.

A shame. Despite being second choice, Teena could have used a little fantasy romance.

Surrounded by her giggling cousins and doing her best to keep her sister from causing disaster, Teena tried to keep her attention away from Dmitri and her dad. But her gaze kept straying, and that was how she ended up not spotting the poor waiter who tried to come alongside her to offer a drink.

Aunt Patty was gracious enough to exclaim, after she got soaked by the white wine spritzers, "Oh don't you fret, dear. I was getting kind of hot anyhow."

But Teena did fret. For all her grace most of the time, it took only one misstep, one whirl, sometimes just one bend over to grab a quarter off the sidewalk, to cause catastrophe.

Her ability to cause mishaps had led to more than one date ditching her, sometimes with the check.

Nothing was more embarrassing than to have a possible beau not return from the washroom after she accidentally squirted lobster juice in his face when she tried to crack a claw.

Now she stuck to easy foods when on a date, but that didn't mean they ended any better, especially considering that, when she wouldn't put out on the first one, or the second one, they rarely returned for a third. Her stance that she would put out only once she was wed had led to a few men crossing her off their list.

Apparently abstinence was too much for them to handle.

The vow she took to remain pure until she met and wedded *the one* meant she was now in her mid twenties and still a virgin, which amused Meena to no end.

"Sis, what the hell are you waiting for?"

A husband. True love. The perfect moment.

An impossible fantasy.

Teena didn't have the same ballsy attitude her sister did. Actually, no one was quite like her twin, Meena, who, with a screech, went after the "bitch" who dared flirt with her new husband.

With a shake of her head, Teena turned away from the carnage and hair pulling. She'd seen it many times before. It never failed to appall her. Mother's lessons on proper behavior just never stuck with Teena's twin.

As for Teena, she did her best to act as a lady should, but at times, she wondered if she shouldn't follow her sister's lead. She seemed to have much more fun.

A shiver went down her spine, a tingle of awareness that gave her only the slightest warning before an accented voice said, "Excuse me, but I don't think we've had the pleasure of meeting."

Whirling, she beheld the jilted Russian. This close, he proved even more formidable and sexy. Few men had the ability to make her feel small. He did, though, the height and breadth of him a perfect complement to her own size. The dark hair, with its hint of tiger orange and gold, appeared soft, and the right length for someone to run their fingers through. A strong nose, defined cheekbones, a square and stubborn chin were offset by full sensual lips, lips that curled into a sensual smile, promising wicked delights.

Intense, bright blue eyes caught her. His scent, a spicy mix of cologne, musk, and man swirled around her in a heady combination that stole her breath for a moment. It also muddled her thoughts.

She blinked at him, rather stupidly, as she tried

to find any kind of words to reply. It took her a good minute, but she managed to a squeak a loquacious, "Hi."

So much for all her lessons on small talk. If she weren't out in the open, she might have found a wall to bang her head against.

"Hello." Oh, how the rumble of his voice thrilled her, but not as much as the smoldering interest in his gaze. She didn't drop her eyes, but only because he mesmerized her. "I am Dmitri."

"I know." Again, the mistress of conversation.

He arched a brow, his lips curved and his cheek hinted at a dimple. Deadly combination. "I see my reputation precedes me."

"Indeed it does, kind of like the stench from a skunk," a lioness of the pride—Luna, a good friend and cousin—interjected as she joined them. "Hate to break it to you, big fella, but everyone knows you're a stalker."

"Stalker? No. More like an admirer."

Teena bit her lip trying not to smile, but it was hard, given he said it with a wink in her direction.

Luna had no such problem when it came to ignoring his flirting. "Don't you be throwing that suave Russian charm around, buddy. Teena is off limits, so bug off."

"How interesting you should say that, as her father just gave me the same warning. Does *Teena*"— and yes he practically purred her name—"not get a say?"

The focus of his gaze, she couldn't stop herself from saying, "I'll decide whom I talk to and hang with." What on earth? Teena wondered if she looked as surprised as she felt. Had she seriously just said that?

Apparently she had, according to the dropped

jaw on Luna and the pleased smile on Dmitri.

"The lady has spoken. You may run along now," he told Luna, smugness in his tone.

The stranger inside Teena spoke again. "The lady says maybe you should hold your tiger, big guy. While I might want the right to make my own decisions on whom I talk to, I never said that included you."

Forget him taking offense at her words, his smile broadened. "Is this your subtle American way of asking me to woo you?"

"I think we all know your method of wooing," Luna muttered darkly. "Kidnapping, locked rooms, and threats aren't the way to get a girlfriend."

"And yet don't the romance novels use these very same methods to gain a hero a bride?"

Teena's forehead furrowed, and she couldn't help but ask, "What would you know about romance novels?"

"It matters not."

Luna snickered. "I think it does. Don't tell me you read romance books?"

Judging by the somewhat ruddy color highlighting his sharp cheekbones, he did. It was so utterly out of character that Teena couldn't help but think it adorable. She jumped to his defense. "I find it commendable that a man is secure enough in his masculinity that he would resort to reading something traditionally considered for women only because he likes it."

He snorted. "I read it in an attempt to understand the morass that is the female mind. Alas, despite emulating the antics of the male heroes in such sagas, I've yet to achieve the same level of success. In other words, I have yet to net the perfect bride."

"Did it ever occur to you that you should try

dating?" Luna sassed. "I realize you're used to blow-up dolls that don't require much attention, but when it comes to real women, they need a little more. Say, like asking her out for dinner, maybe listen to her talk, do nice things for her like open doors and buy her flowers, not abduct her and make her a prisoner in your dungeon."

"For your information, I did not keep her in a dungeon. It was a tower."

For some reason, Teena found this eminently funny. She snickered. Then giggled. "That would explain Meena's complaint that she wished she had Rapunzel's hair."

"As if she needed it. My men and I are still baffled as to how she managed to escape that room. The lock should have been foolproof."

Teena shrugged. "She's always been handy that way."

"And are you the same? Do you know how to pick locks and hotwire motorcycles?"

"No. But I can knit." Her lame skill didn't make him laugh. On the contrary, he seemed entirely too pleased.

"Good to know."

Luna shoved a finger in his chest. "Oh no it's not. You will not kidnap her like you did Meena. Teena's too sweet to know how to escape you, which means we'd have to come and kick your ass when we rescue her."

The lack of faith her friend had in her burned. Teena wasn't that incompetent, and who said she'd want saving? There was something rather darkly delicious about Dmitri's casual assurance and domineering manner.

If only I weren't second choice.

Puffing his chest, Dmitri fixed Luna with a regal stare. "Who says Teena would want rescuing? I am an eligible male, of impeccable breeding, exceeding wealth, and—"

"Lots of arrogance," Teena added with a shake of her head. "Luna's right. I think you should find someone else to focus your attention on." Funny how the very suggestion made her inner lioness growl while the woman in her drooped in disappointment

She wilted even further when he said, "As you wish," and walked away.

It wasn't just her inner feline that made the sad meowing sound.

Guess I wasn't worth the trouble after all.

Chapter Three

Stubborn women were the bane of Dmitri's existence, and it seemed fate enjoyed tossing them constantly in his path. Especially when it came to settling down with a woman.

Upon meeting Teena, he'd hoped she would prove easy to charm and hoped she would find herself as intrigued by him as he was of her. But no. She ordered him to leave her alone, and he left.

Stalking away went against his upbringing. Russian nobility, even the shifter kind, didn't admit defeat. Teethed on adversity by a mother who didn't understand the meaning of losing meant Dmitri didn't give up. Winning was the only option. Yet, even the most famous general knew when to retreat and regroup, especially in delicate situations, such as this one.

Surrounded by the enemy, also known as her bloody, well-meaning family, he had to tread cautiously. None of them wanted him to steal the luscious Teena. But their opinion didn't matter for he'd seen a glimmer of hope.

Upon their meeting, Dmitri had sensed Teena's interest, an interest made impossible to pursue due to the intervention of a meddling lioness. Given Luna seemed determined to thwart him, he left Teena with her chaperone, but he didn't abandon his plot.

On the contrary, his interest was piqued. As soon as he heard her speak, and caught a whiff of her delectable scent—woman, all woman with a hint of vanilla—he became determined to make her his. The threat by her father to kill him didn't bother him. Some things were worth endangering one's life for.

Like his little kitten.

Yummy curves.

His inner feline was right. She did tempt with a delectable shape, more womanly than Meena's, who possessed a more athletic type body.

Dmitri liked a more full-figured woman. This woman.

She will be mine.

And to hell—of which he was part owner, given no one wanted the deed to land in Northern Russia—with anyone who thought to stand in his way. He would have her, and before the end of the night.

Of course it took some maneuvering. No one trusted the Russian, or so he overheard. At least the men didn't. The women, however, fluttered their lashes and sighed as they chattered about his "dangerous mien" and "determined nature."

Determined was right. They also missed suave, sly, and seductive, all tools he planned to put to use in wooing the luscious lady whom he couldn't keep his eyes from.

Waiting until Teena found herself alone took some time. Eventually, however, her guard cat wandered off to dance while Teena watched longingly from the sidelines. Approaching with a pair of drinks, he offered her one. "Might I offer you refreshment?"

"I shouldn't. Mother says to never accept a drink from a stranger."

"Ah, but we are not strangers."

"That's right. You're my sister's ex stalker."

"So harshly you judge me, and yet, perhaps you

should perceive things from my perspective. I saw a woman I wanted and went after her."

"You went after my sister."

"Obviously a mistake."

"You think?" Her lips tilted in a smirk.

"Yes, I do think it was a mistake because she pales in comparison to you."

That made her giggle, the sound light and natural. "Oh, that's good. But it won't work. Fact is my sister dumped you, and I won't be the rebound girl."

"Shot down without given a chance. You wound me, little kitten." He attempted to appear aggrieved.

"Little?" She snorted. "Now you're really laying it on thick."

"Next to me you are little." To prove his point, he invaded her space. To his delight, she didn't move but allowed him close, close enough for him to truly surround himself in her essence.

Ambrosia.

Want her. Take her.

Not exactly feasible given they had an audience, but he almost said screw it, especially when the tip of her pink tongue licked her lips.

"Anyone ever mention you're a huge flirt?" Said in a breathy voice that matched the rapid flutter of her pulse.

"There is nothing wrong with showing admiration for a woman."

"Except I hear your admiration is less about a woman's scintillating personality and more about the width of her hips."

"I am a practical man. My future mate must be able to handle a male of my *stature.*" He purred the word at her, loving how her pupils dilated and the musk of her arousal surrounded him.

"You want super babies."

"I want a family. A wife. A future. Are those things really so wrong?"

"No." She whispered the word as she stared at him. For a moment, he thought she would kiss him. Or should he kiss her, audience be damned?

Her lips parted, and her eyes stared into his with a sultry intensity that mesmerized.

She leaned forward, chin tilted, soft breath fluttering between them—

A raucous yell interrupted them, "Here come the Jell-O shots."

Snapped from their intimate trance, she reared back and dropped her gaze. "You can't decide your future based on the circumference of a woman's hips."

"Perhaps not, but I can definitely succumb to admiration of her witty repartee, the sensual allure of her body, and the desire she evokes with merely the slightest purse of her lips." Where the poet in him came from he couldn't have said. Dmitri never resorted to flowery flirtation. His commanding presence was usually all that was required. Yet, with Teena, he found himself dazzled. Beneath her shy exterior lurked a quick-witted mind, a sassy sense of humor, and a backbone when it came to retaining her pride.

However, he should note, before he had to resort to violence to reassert his manhood, that, beneath all those emotions, strongest of all was pure, unadulterated lust.

Gentle words didn't mean his fantasy pandered softly. Teena's dress provoked more carnal thoughts than that. In his fantasy, she'd have her hands braced on a wall, facing it, her buttocks outthrust in invitation. He could so easily see his hands sliding the silk of that skirt over plump and creamy thighs. Would she wear full-bottomed undergarments or something skimpier?

Her eyes widened. "Did you just growl?"

"Consider it an outward expression of my admiration for your assets."

"I think enough people have told you these assets are off limits."

She repeated it, and yet, he didn't sense any conviction in the words. *Of course she doesn't mean it. She is mine. She knows it. Now I just need for her to admit it.*

He tried the direct approach. "There is no use in fighting it. You are mine."

"Excuse me?"

"You. Are. Mine." He enunciated it very distinctly.

"You are crazy." She tossed the insult and yet couldn't hide the heat radiating from her body.

"I am Russian." Although, to many, there wasn't much of a difference.

"You do know, if you try anything, you'll have my family to contend with."

"Are you doing this on purpose to entice me?"

"How is the fact that my father would kill you and feed your body to the gators enticing?"

"Danger does not sway me. A man does not get to my position without encountering a few battles on the way. No worthy prize comes without a price."

"Funny, you didn't think your life was worth the price with your last fiancée or she wouldn't be upstairs right now enjoying her honeymoon."

"That is because she was not you. You are my mate."

Her breath caught, and her eyes widened. Why this seemed to shake her he couldn't have said.

Flustered, finally, she snatched at the wine glass

in his hand, but she left it untouched and turned her gaze toward the people dancing.

For a moment, nothing was said. As she pretended interest in the gyrating bodies, he studied her.

While he couldn't help but think of her as a little kitten beside him, the truth was Teena towered over most women, even in her bare feet, but he stood taller still.

Since they stood side by side, he noted the top of her head resided just below his nose. A wondrous height. A perfect height that would allow him to simply dip his head to touch those precious lips.

With her head angled away from him, he got to admire the smooth ski slope of her nose, the tilt on the end adorable, as were the smattering of pale freckles across it. He couldn't determine the length of her golden-hued locks, bound as they were in a chignon atop her head, but he could see the silky sheen and imagine their texture from the fat ringlets draping her face.

As she stared at the dancers, she didn't move when he reached out to toy with a corkscrewed strand. "I can see you want to dance. Why do you not join them?" The idea of seeing her move in time to the rhythm, hips undulating, body swaying... He could only hope to control himself at the sight.

She shook her head, and her expression turned woebegone. "I can't go out there. While I might like to dance, it is best done when I'm alone. Fewer people get injured that way."

"Surely it's not that bad," he teased as he took a sip of his wine.

"It's worse," she said with a grimace. She grimaced again when she sipped at the wine. "Oh please don't tell me you got the stuff from the brown bottles?"

"The ones with no label? It was the beta of this pride who recommended it."

"Because Hayder obviously doesn't like you. This is Uncle Joe's homemade stuff. Only the truly taste bud dead or masochist type drink it."

In other words, the toughest.

Dmitri took another sip. "I rather like it. It has a certain pungent, earthy taste that reminds me of home. It is somewhat bold, and daring, but completely real and unabashed."

"All that from one taste?"

"One you did not appreciate. Try it again and, this time, hold it in your mouth. Let the flavors burst upon your tongue." Much like he longed to burst within her. By all the hairy gods—that his grandmother liked to talk about and worship, despite his mother's exasperated sighs—she drew him.

"Do I have to?" She eyed the wine in her glass dubiously.

"Yes."

"Aren't you afraid I'll spit it on you?"

"Spit or swallow, the choice is yours." Innuendo totally understood—and intentional.

Cheeks red, she didn't reply but stared at the glass in her hand. Nose wrinkled, Teena sniffed the wine and took another gulp. She held it in her mouth and cocked her head to the side as she followed his instructions before swallowing it with a shy smile in his direction.

He'd never seen anything more cock hardening. And then laughable as she made a face.

"Nope. Still god-awful."

Husky laughter shook him. "Perhaps it is my

Russian heritage that allows me to admire the work that went into it. Might I fetch you something sweeter for your palate?"

He saw her about to say no, ready to refuse him, except she didn't. Straightening her spine and giving him a bright smile, she said, "I'd like that, please."

Thus did he fetch her a margarita, the rim crusted with sugar. Worst idea ever tied with best idea ever. That lithe pink tongue slid forth more than once to lap at the treat, pure torture and invitation to fantasy, as he could so easily imagine licking the seam of her lips to taste the sweetness.

Since he doubted he could resist her if she kept doing it, he next fetched her a lemonade cooler, the pucker of the citrus making Teena's nose wrinkle adorably. He didn't get the impression she was a big drinker, and yet, she allowed him to feed her glass after glass. Even more marvelous, despite the pointed signals from several people, including her own father—who spent a good portion of the evening glaring at them— Teena conversed with him.

He mentioned it at one point. "You have yet to walk away, despite the urgings of your friends."

"What do you mean?" she asked, finger rolling through the condensation pooling on the bottle she held with slim fingers.

"Your father has yet to move his gaze from you."

"He's a tad overprotective."

"I rather admire that about him. The head of the family should look after those in his charge."

"That's archaic."

He smiled. "It's tradition."

"Another Russian thing?"

He replied with a rolled shoulder. "It is how I am. How my father was and my grandfather." It was also the motto drilled into him by his mother and grandmother. *Family always comes first. Kill the rest.* His family didn't have a gentle past.

"You say that, and yet you respect my father's warning so much you haven't left my side."

"How else am I to court you?"

"And are you courting me?"

Words weren't needed in that moment, just a slow, sensual smile that dropped her gaze and brought a pink glow to her cheeks.

The ambiance around them shifted as a slow song finally materialized among the seemingly non-stop thunderous beat. A smooth, sensual rhythm that insisted on being used.

Setting down his bottle, he grabbed the one she held by the long neck and also placed it to the side. He clasped her empty hand and drew her toward the dance floor, even as she asked, "What are you doing?"

"What does it look like we are doing?"

"Heading into the danger zone."

"Such melodrama. Relax, little kitten, we will simply dance." Dance dressed and upright for the moment.

"Dance? With me? Oh no, you don't want to do that."

Yet the shake of her head, which loosed a few more fat golden curls, did not sway him. Dmitri was possessed of a powerful urge to hold her in his arms, to fit her against him and...probably start a fight.

Up until now, those chaperoning her seemed lenient. However, should he stray across a boundary, diplomatic guest or not, he didn't doubt they'd act.

The danger didn't make him hesitate one bit.

Nor did he pay heed to her feeble protest. Reaching the center of the crowd, which parted before his demanding glare, he turned her to face him.

With one hand clasping hers, the other at her waist, he began a slow, simple waltz that, at first, she hesitated to follow.

She tried one last protest. "You really don't want to do this."

He didn't think she tread on his foot on purpose. "We are dancing, little kitten, so you might as well hush and enjoy it."

"Don't say I didn't warn you," was her ominous reply.

While her words promised one thing, her actual reaction proved the opposite. As they moved in a four step, her body lost its rigid tenseness, limbs loosening, her movements falling in line with his. Their tempo matched, their bodies synchronized.

Dmitri added some flair to their steps, and to his delight, she adapted, her hips swiveling, her feet stepping, and her smile beaming while her eyes lit with enjoyment.

He chose to ignore that their wild movements caused some people to dart out of the way. That was their own fault for dancing too close to a pair of suns because, yes, in his mind, they were both quite brilliant.

Again, not arrogance, just plain fact.

How delightful she appeared, her lips tilted into a smile of enjoyment. A rosy flush in her cheeks, a soft laugh escaped through parted lips, all spoke to her enjoyment. Her nearness aroused, even if their dance wasn't body to body. It didn't need to be that close when the elegance of their movements and the pull of her gaze aroused him more than should have been feasible.

Electricity danced between them, sparking the air with delightful suspense, and yes, he'd dare say it, lust.

It might seem too crass to compare, and yet he couldn't help himself, given touching Teena lit him on fire while being around Meena usually meant he was holding himself ready to move. She sure didn't hit like a girl.

Teena, on the other hand, was all woman. Seductive curves, entrancing scent, and to the idiot who got her foot in his face when Dmitri dipped, "Next time move out of the lady's way," Dmitri growled when the fool opened his mouth, about to whine. The guy slunk away.

Pussy.

He offered a glare to anyone else in the vicinity that might mar his enjoyment. Dmitri was dancing with his lady, and no one had better interrupt.

The slow song migrated to something with a quicker tempo. He changed their steps yet again, and for a moment, she matched him, a brisk shake of her hips—dear gods! He could have carried her off when, with a shy smile, she added a dash of seduction.

No more was Teena content for his hand to guide her waist. Nor did she want to clasp fingers. She draped her arms around his neck, invading his space.

I surrender.

In that moment, Dmitri was hers. And she was his.

"Mine."

"What did you say?" She danced only a few hairsbreadths from him, and her soft query tickled his skin.

Did he dare repeat himself? *I fear nothing. Not even the truth.* "I said you are mine." As he said the words, he angled his hips away and braced for impact.

Teena didn't attempt to knee him. Or punch him. Nor did she insult him like Meena—*"The only way I'll ever belong to you is if you kill me and stuff me like some trophy."* Despite her splendid hips, he found himself tempted to do so.

But not with Teena. With this woman, he enjoyed himself, finding her gracious in her talk, addictive with her laughter, and an utter goddess when she danced in his arms. Even if they didn't quite touch, heat radiated, burning him.

Would he combust if there was nothing to separate their skin?

Stripping not being conducive to the moment, he satisfied himself with tugging her close and placing his hands on her waist. Flush against him, she danced, still not as close as he'd like. His hands slid down until they cupped the sweet curve of her ass.

Squeeze. A perfect fit in his palms.

This close together, she couldn't miss his desire. His erection pulsed and strained, it hinted, quite strongly, that they should find somewhere private so he could sheath himself within her. He wanted her naked, beneath him, her eyes closed and head tilted, her mouth rounded in panting pleasure. He wanted her creamy thighs wrapped around him, helping him to sink deep into her glorious body. He'd wager some of the same thoughts teased her as well, given her musky arousal swirled around him in a heady mix.

She wants. She's ours.

He tilted her chin, but her gaze wouldn't meet his.

"Look at me, little kitten. See and feel how you affect me." He pressed her as firmly as he could against him.

She drew in a breath, peered up at him, and—

Later he would blame all the blood in his brain that vacated for not recalling they were in a very public place, a place inhabited by his enemies who didn't take too kindly to the liberties he took with a certain lady on the dance floor. Perhaps, had his dick left a little red stuff to power his mind, he would have also noticed a certain father bearing down on them with murder in his eyes.

It was certainly his dick's fault that the fist caught him square in the jaw. It didn't fell him, but it certainly stung. Not that he rubbed it or said a word aloud. Men didn't whine in public—they waited to tell their mother later so she could rant at length about the disrespect of peasants and plot ways to ruin them.

But in this case, he didn't need mother dear. And even better, he wouldn't have to destroy Peter and thus mar the beginning of his new life with Teena. Not optimism. Fact. She would be his.

Yet, why earn her ire by killing Peter when she seemed determined to berate her father on her own?

"What are you doing?" she demanded as she placed herself between them.

"Move out of the way, baby girl. I need to get that foreign furball to show you some respect."

"He was being a perfect gentleman, unlike certain meddling parents," she snapped with a show of spirit Dmitri enjoyed and yet seemed to surprise her father.

"He was mauling you."

"And I was enjoying it!"

A sudden silence descended just as Teena shouted it. However, Dmitri could have applauded when, despite her red cheeks, she tilted her chin and remained facing her father.

The big man looked flummoxed. "I was just looking out for you. He's a no-good foreigner who's just using you because he can't have your sister."

Oooh. That stung.

Dmitri didn't need to hear Teena's indrawn breath to know the words hurt. Teena spun on her heel and marched off.

Peter appeared dumbstruck, but only for a moment, before he took off after her. "Baby girl, I didn't mean it like that. You know you're perfect."

As Dmitri watched them stalk away, he noted it was probably prudent not to follow. Let Teena hash it out with her father. While he waited for them to complete their spat, Dmitri could bask in the fact that she'd stood up for them.

Them. As in a duo. How astonishing that, in his pursuit of one woman, he'd found the one he was truly meant to be with.

Now to convince her of that fact.

Luna returned, probably with a new plan to thwart him or an insult tailored for him. Her verbal attacks made him nostalgic for home. "I'll call you a liar if you tell this to her dad, but you guys were kind of cute dancing together. I mean there were a couple of incidents, like when Teena accidentally tripped the dude coming to cut in on you, but overall, I'd call it a success."

"She dances like an angel." Light as a feather and more beautiful.

Ack. Was that his tiger hacking a hairball at his ridiculous poetic side that kept regurgitating the oddest things? At least it was only about Teena.

"But she only dances like that with you. Imagine that."

Why imagine when he knew it was fate?

Teena was his mate. Or would be as soon as he could get her away from her family. What was a tiger to do?

Stalk, of course.

Rawr.

Chapter Four

Teena stalked off, her blood boiling but for so many reasons. Peeved at her dad, a little peeved at herself, and aroused, damn him.

While they were talking, she'd managed to forget Dmitri was a poor choice. As they danced, she could think only of how good it felt. How right.

How fated…?

Given Meena had recently explained to her how it felt to know she'd met the one, Teena had to wonder.

His appearance hit her in the chest each time, a powerful blow that made her breathing stutter, her heart pound madly, and the most delicious heat to invade her.

She liked Dmitri.

She desired Dmitri.

He's ours, said her lioness.

But as Daddy reminded her, she was only second best.

It stung. It stung more than it should have but only because it was so true. Dmitri was using her as a replacement. Despite all his pretty words and claims, the fact remained that she was second choice.

And she hated it.

In that moment she might have even hated her sister.

Why couldn't we have met first?

Her father chased after her, his "Baby girl,

don't you walk away from me," not helping her plaintive tantrum.

She whirled, eyes bright with tears but voice steady as she said, "I will do what I want. I am a grown woman."

"A grown woman that I'm trying to stop from making a mistake. I know that Russian fellow seems sincere and whatnot, but we know what he's after."

"A replacement." Bitterly said, her lips tightening.

"I was going to say good genes."

"Whatever. Apparently it's too much to believe that, while he might have come after me because I've got big hips, perhaps he hung out with me all night because, hey, maybe I'm kind of fun."

"Sure he did."

She didn't like the placating tone in his voice at all. "Are you implying I'm boring?"

"No, of course not."

"Yes you are because I'm not as wild as Meena or outspoken as Luna. Or thinking that every situation needs a violent resolution."

"Violence is more efficient," her father grumbled.

"Don't change the subject. The fact of the matter is, whether Dmitri is playing me or not, it isn't for you or Luna or anyone else to decide. It's my choice if I want to listen to him compliment me or tell him about my third grade trip." Which had resulted in her and Meena getting banned from the zoo...for life. "I was having fun. It didn't mean I was about to elope with him." Although she did have a very Meena thought along the lines of *Wait a second, wouldn't mother have a kitten if I did?* As for her father, she could only imagine the swath of destruction.

A pity she didn't have the guts to do it.

This was assuming that Dmitri truly meant what he said, that he wanted her. Thing was, could she look past being second place?

I was until someone pointed it out to me.

And all this was moot.

Dmitri would probably steer a wide berth now given the antics of her family.

I wish they'd trust me more. She hadn't made it to her ripe age still a virgin because she fell for false flattery.

Given she wasn't in the mood to dance anymore—in her state she'd probably cause some serious harm—she began to head back to the house, only she got waylaid on the way by a pair of ugly cousins, a few times removed, who insisted they share a drink.

While not much of a drinker, the Jell-O shots went down nicely as she bitched about her father to anyone who would listen.

After the fourth—or was it the fifth?—cherry-flavored gelatin mouthful, she felt herself wobbling on her feet.

Damn, she'd drunk way more than she was used to. Time to say goodnight and find her bed. She waved goodbye to the women she'd talked to and weaved her way to the house. As she tottered, and prepared to say hello to the ground—face first—an arm caught her. Snaring her around the waist, Dmitri reeled her upright and held her there.

A good thing he held them steady because the world around them spun. Dammit, that was taking the whole world-revolves-around-me axiom a little too far.

"Careful, little kitten. The ground is a hard place to land."

"So is your chest," she sassed back then giggled.

"So you noticed."

Since she leaned against said chest, she felt him puff it out. The alcohol making her bold, she placed her hand over his heart while her head cradled just under his chin. "I noticed a lot of things about you. But the one thing I can't figure out is if you're telling the truth." She, on the other hand, was apparently drunk enough to not hide her curiosity.

"The truth about what, little kitten?"

"How do I know you want me for me?"

"Is not the fact that we're still here talking and not on a plane for Russia with a priest indication that I am willing to woo you?"

She blinked. It took a moment to process his words. "You're wooing?"

"Well, yes. That is generally the step one takes to convince a woman to marry him."

"You want to marry me?"

"But of course. You are mine."

"And you can decide this in just one night?" It sounded kind of familiar. Hadn't he proposed after one date to her sister? Ugh. Déjà vu. "I gotta go."

She broke free of his loose embrace and spun on a bare heel, tottered, and almost fell.

Once again, he was there to catch her.

"I see you are overwhelmed, little kitten."

"No. I'm annoyed at myself for thinking you liked me. And even more annoyed that my dad was right. I'm nothing to you but a breeding machine. Good night, Dmitri. Have a safe trip back to Russia. Alone."

A little of the fog cleared in her head as she strode away from him. If you could call one stride leaving.

Except he wasn't ready to let her go.

He placed himself in front of her, cupped her cheeks, and forced her to face him. "I will prove you mean more," were the words he whispered just before he slanted his mouth over hers.

Sizzling electricity arced between them, the touch of his lips on her a shock, a good one.

Forget pushing him away, forget everything but the feel of him nipping and tugging at her lower lip. Basking in the seductive pleasure of his tongue, she clung to him as he quested within the warm recess of her mouth.

A strange languor invaded her limbs. She went limp in his arms. But still he kissed her, hunger in his bold strokes, heat in his cupping hands.

No bones to hold her up.

Literally.

More than just passion made her legs buckle and her eyes shut, the lassitude in her body a result of her drunken state and not his touch. Or was there more to it?

Am I drugged?

Did he do it?

Good grief, was she about to become a tiger's bride?

A spurt of elation and fear then…

Darkness fell like a curtain over her mind.

Chapter Five

Dmitri had made women swoon in the past.

For example, Petra, who belonged to his grandmother's crib club, had hit the rug upon seeing him in all his glory. And he meant naked glory. Not intentionally, though. He'd gone for a run through the woods and returned to find the house servants had cleared his scattered clothes.

Apparently, gray hair and a few wrinkles didn't mean the old ladies didn't admire a man in his prime. But he could have done without the pinches by those who remained alert.

Dmitri had also made people faint with a simple, pointed glare. Those low on the totem of power never could handle his majestic stare of displeasure.

But Teena... Teena swooned from his kiss.

And she snored.

He didn't know whether to roar and wake her up or keep staring in stunned disbelief.

Women didn't succumb to boredom during his embraces. Especially not the woman meant for him.

A light shake didn't rouse her. Her eyes remained shut, and her thick golden lashes, lightly coated with mascara, fluttered against her cheeks.

Now what?

He was at a complete loss as to what to do next. He couldn't very well carry her to his room—with its bed and privacy and... He could just imagine the lynch mob if he did that, and with good reason, considering the debauchery that could happen.

Forget taking her to her room. Again, no one would ever believe he wouldn't take advantage.

A bad-ass reputation was sometimes a hindrance.

What did that leave? He couldn't simply abandon her here on the ground, at the mercy of anyone, alone and unguarded.

No one must touch. Guard our woman. Even his tiger knew that was a bad idea.

Sigh. Only one thing to do, since kidnapping her was probably also out of the question—these lions were such spoilsports. He sat. Cross-legged on the ground, he draped her body across his lap and held her cradled. It was oddly intimate, even if he was the only one conscious for it.

It also didn't go unnoticed.

Luna, wearing a suspicious scowl, soon confronted him.

"What the hell are you doing with my girl Teena?"

"Trying to be a gentleman, which I'll admit is very taxing. I do not know how the heroic types do it all the time." Keeping his hands to himself when so many curves beckoned took willpower.

Crouching down alongside him, Luna cocked her head before saying, "You're a weird dude."

"The correct term is noble *boyar*, or you could call me prince."

She snickered. "Next thing I know, you'll be wanting us to add charming and trying to convince Teena she's your Snow White."

"Do you think my kiss would wake her?" A proud kind of guy, he didn't admit it was a kiss that had bored her to sleep in the first place.

"I don't know, and I don't think you should try."

"Are you about to lecture me on staying away again?" He couldn't help a roll of his eyes.

"No, I wasn't going to tell you take a hike. Actually, I think you should stick around for a bit."

Almost did Dmitri drop Teena, his shock was so great. "Stay? Why? So you can better plan how to cause my demise? Do you need time to fetch some rope and find a tree?"

"Oh, we don't need time for that. Uncle Peter's already got something all mapped out. Auntie's roses will fetch a fine price this year if he goes through with it. But, no, that's not why I think you should stay. If you're truly serious about Teena—"

"I am." Spoken with the utmost truth.

"Then you can prove it by dating her. You know, do things in a normal fashion. Show her family that she's not just a set of hips. Give Teena the chance to really get to know you. If this is real and meant to be, then—"

"When I ask her to marry me, she shall agree, and I will have my bride."

"If she agrees."

"Oh, she'll agree." He knew it, didn't harbor a single doubt, which was why he handed his lovely little kitten off to Luna and some other cousins, who promised to put her to bed. His utmost faith that she would fall madly in love with him was why he sent a text to his henchmen cancelling the plans he'd made during the ceremony to kidnap her.

Off to bed he went, pleased with himself, and the world. Even the guard outside his door couldn't ruin his fine mood.

Guard me all you want. I'll be here in the morning, wooing my bride.

Or at least, that was what he planned to do. Fate had other ideas. It seemed the ranch had sporadic cellular signal, which meant his last text never reached his men.

Chapter Six

Awareness came with the speed of cold honey spooling from a dangling spoon. Slowly. So slowly, and that was why it took the third time for her to grasp someone spoke.

"Say I do."

"Hunh?" Eyes closed, and the lids too heavy to lift, her mouth a fuzzy peach in need of water, Teena's mind struggled to wake from the most molasses sleep ever.

"Say I do," hissed an accented voice, a voice that seemed familiar. But it was the scent that made her smile. Manly musk intermixed with a spicy cologne. It seemed her Russian admirer was still at her side. Had she fallen asleep on him at the party?

It was so hard to remember.

"Repeat after me. I. Do."

What did she do? Forcing her brain into gear, she strove to recall events. Last she remembered, she was weaving back to the house after her sister's wedding—drunk as hell because she was so mad at her interfering family—when Dmitri, that sexy Russian, waylaid her. He'd made sure the ground didn't get fresh with her body parts. Instead, he let them get fresh with his solid frame.

He held her in his arms. Said stuff. Nice stuff. But forget that and fast forward to the exciting part where he kissed her.

Oh my. Upon her he bestowed a masterful kiss

that melted her. She remembered the sense of weakness in her limbs. The roam of his hands, then...?

Her brow wrinkled. She couldn't recollect anything past the amazing kiss.

Nothing. At all.

Had she seriously fallen asleep during the most intense embrace of her life?

Was this why Dmitri held her in his arms, his musky scent surrounding her? "Wake, little kitten. Just for a moment. I need you to say I do."

"I do?" Do what? Surely he didn't demand permission to kiss her again? Was he after something else? Blerg. She wished her brain wasn't such a sluggish mess.

Giving her cobwebbed thoughts a mental shake, she pried her eyes open in time to see Dmitri's handsome face hovering close to hers. She also heard the words, "I now pronounce you man and wife. You may kiss the bride."

What!

Before she could grasp what had happened, lips pressed against hers in a molten touch that melted her questions and awakened a fire. The kiss didn't help her regain her senses. On the contrary, she slipped into a pleasurable state with only one real thought in mind—more.

More kisses. More heat. More Dmitri.

The arms wrapped around her body held her upright and a good thing, too, seeing as how her legs had the consistency of soft rubber. A tiny part of her remarked she should protest, or at least make an effort to assert some kind of control.

She wasn't firing on all cylinders. A sluggishness still held her. It occurred to her she should cry and be frightened, and yet...

She truly was enjoying the soft mesh of lips and the warmth of his breath. Or she was until she found herself deposited in a chair. Talk about a rude awakening.

Her body lamented the loss of the warmth from his while her inner lioness meowed in frustration. A frustration she understood all too well, given the ardor he woke refused to settle so easily.

Struggling against the lassitude in her body, she managed to flutter her eyes open, not that it helped her comprehension much. She didn't recognize her surroundings.

A pen was pushed into her hands. "Sign here," Dmitri's accented voice purred in her ear.

"What is it?" she muttered through numb lips as she struggled to remain awake. She peered blearily at the white sheet in front of her, to no avail. The words on the paper wavered.

"It is what you want."

Truly? Because...*I want him.*

Without giving it a second thought, she signed.

Then he did too, using the same pen she had, his bold signature alongside hers on the marriage certificate.

Blink.

Re-read.

Nope, the words on the paper hadn't change.

She stabbed a finger at the paper, not trusting herself to speak. But if she had, it might have sounded a lot like her father, but with fewer swear words. *What the fuck just happened?*

He answered her unspoken question. "We are husband and wife, little kitten."

Oh my. How unexpected.

Married. She was married. To Dmitri. *I am*

married to the tiger.

Hunh, a coerced wedding, a first for the family and certainly never a disaster her sister had ever managed.

Point for me?

No, because Meena evaded Dmitri's plans.

I, on the other hand, fell like a domino. Worse, I didn't see it coming. I really thought he liked me. Thought he'd meant it when he said he would woo her and prove his intent.

What a jerk, kidnapping her like this and marrying her on the sly. Making her his wife.

His wife?

Could a lioness giggle? Her inner feline certainly seemed a tad too pleased.

His mate. The mental rumble vibrated through her body like a ghostly purr, one that left her senses alive.

Are you going to stand up and assert your rights?

"You can't force me to marry you. Tell him." She addressed the latter to the man dressed in a suit with a clerical collar of black and white, some kind of religious guy. Surely he wouldn't condone this farce. "Tell him it doesn't count because I didn't agree."

"You said I do," Dmitri reminded her.

"Because you told me to while I wasn't even awake. It doesn't count. And why is that priest ignoring me?"

"Little kitten, if you calm down, we can—"

"I will not calm down." She lunged from the chair, only belatedly realizing the flimsiness of it.

The plastic bucket chair with its metal legs, a relic from the seventies, cracked. The hand she'd used to push off slid as the plastic snapped, and she lost her balance. Tipping sideways, she threw out her hand, but her reflexes were still kind of woozy and she missed, hitting the floor with her shoulder then a ricochet of her head. Damned industrial marble floor.

She lay there, at an angle, stunned, and also exposing a lot more leg than she should. Through squinted eyes, she noted her skirt riding high on her hip.

Dmitri noticed too. Interest smoldered in his gaze, a gaze stolen by the collared man, who cleared his throat.

How dare he steal Dmitri's attention?

Grrrr.

Who growled?

"Now, now, little kitten, give me a moment to deal with this obviously brave man, daring your vicious rage."

"I am not vicious." Vicious was her sister.

"I think you're tougher than you know."

He's right.

Pounce him and give him some licks. Inner kitty just couldn't keep her giant nose out of it. But she wasn't alone in appreciating the compliment.

With a flourish, the marriage license was whisked away and sealed in a brown envelope.

"Make sure you file it today," Dmitri ordered as he handed a wad of green bills to the priest. "I trust there is enough there to maintain your discretion."

"Always a pleasure doing business with your family," the man replied.

"Business? This is illegal," she shouted, kind of annoyed at both of them for their blasé attitude.

"Women. You can't live with them," the collared man grumbled, "and you can't kill them without doing time. And they wonder why I joined the church."

"A man needs heirs, legal ones if he's to leave behind a legacy." Dmitri saw the man to a metal door and let him out.

It was then she noted it was the only door in the room, although the term *room* was being generous.

Getting to her feet gave a full perspective, not that there was truly much to see.

The gray walls screamed utility space, as did the scarred white table, orange smudges, black rings, and scratches forever ruining the pristine surface. Around the table was scattered an odd medley of chairs. As if regurgitated from the seventies, orange plastic bucket seats, mixed with some dark blue and a few lime green ones, were haphazardly scattered.

The one she'd broken lay in two pieces on the floor. It served as a reminder that even while sitting trouble couldn't leave her alone.

While a part of her seemed to think she should lay her head down for a nap—yawn—she knew that wasn't a good plan. Even her woozy thoughts recognized a few important facts.

One, alcohol hadn't caused her slumber. She was drugged!

Two, she was freaking married.

And three, damn, those were some good drugs because, even though she should have been pissed with Dmitri, she just wanted to kiss him.

Get closer. Touch him. Rub against him. Mark him with our scent.

So insidious proved the purred thoughts that she took a step toward him. Only one, and then she froze with the reminder that kissing him was a bad idea.

Good girls behaved. Naughty boys didn't.

And totally alpha male tigers thrived on doing the unbelievable.

Dmitri moved, and quickly, because, the next thing she knew, she was pressed against the front of him.

"Be angry, little kitten. I encourage you to rant and rave."

Confused, she stared at him. "You want me to give you hell? You admit you were wrong?"

"No. I told you that you would be mine, and I kept my promise. But your anger is becoming. Did you know your eyes flash in the most provocative way? And your scent..." He inhaled deeply and closed his eyes. When they reopened, they appeared to glow with the heat of his hunger.

She swallowed. "This isn't a joke."

"I wasn't laughing."

"Yet you're acting so blasé about it all. You kidnapped me and then married me while I was practically still drooling with sleep."

"You snore, not drool."

"Thanks for letting me know," she snapped, not happy that he pointed out an obvious flaw.

"It is cute. I, on the other hand, don't snore."

"Not information I need since we won't be sleeping together."

Her retort saw him chuckling. "You're right. We won't be getting much sleep."

She didn't need the wink to understand the innuendo. As his wife, she could take that next step. His hands gripped her waist, keeping her pressed against the hardness of his body, a torturous cushion for her hyper-aware senses.

"I will make a good husband."

Startled by his announcement, her gaze met his, and her breath hitched. Those intense blue eyes never failed to capture her. Those lips tempted, especially now that she knew their taste, their feel, oh and let her not forget the delight.

A rumble shivered his frame. What perturbed him?

Apparently, she did.

"You must not eye me like that, little kitten. It makes a man want to risk his life and explore the temptation you offer in that gaze."

"How is it risky? A kiss can't kill." Although a lack of one might cause her to self-combust.

"Risky because we don't have time. We must move before those seeking us catch up."

"Who's after us?" she asked. Did Dmitri have enemies? As a mobster in his homeland, surely he had his fair share.

"Your family is on the prowl. Who else? Your father has eyes and ears everywhere. It is damned impressive. I shall have to interrogate him, um, I mean ask my new father-in-law how he does it at a later date. For the moment, I think it best we not step on that lion's tail."

"Scared of my daddy?" Yes, she totally smirked that sassy retort.

"No, just not keen to start my marriage off with the murder of your father. I can see that causing a small issue."

"Small?"

He laughed. "You are right, little kitten. Even if I did kill your father, then you would still adore me madly. But no need to test that theory. We'll leave on my jet as soon as it's fueled."

"We're in an airport?" She cast her gaze around, looking for an indication of which airport. Any kind of escape was good. She couldn't stay married to this madman—even if he had seductive blue eyes and dark charm.

"Us, in an airport? Nope." He stretched the word and made an attempt to look innocent. It totally failed, given he was part devil. Not managing didn't mean the attempted result wasn't ridiculously distracting.

She pulled out of his arms, and he let her. She turned away. *Don't let him suck you into his imaginary world where this kind of thing is normal.* Then again, hadn't he admitted he took his actions from romance novels? Argh. She needed to stop finding the hot in his actions. Escape should remain her focus. "We are in an airport, which means, if I scream for help, someone will come."

Way to give away your plan. Did she want to fail? Did subconsciously she want to remain with Dmitri and see what would happen?

Duh. It seemed her inner feline knew the score.

"I wouldn't recommend drawing notice to yourself."

"Or you'll what?" she dared, a flash of courage emboldening her.

"Kiss you goodnight."

And he did. Spinning her back to face him, he kissed her with breathtaking hunger, with a mouth both hard and soft, demanding yet coaxing.

He *owned* her in that moment. Right then and there, she would have followed him everywhere, but when she felt the prick of a needle in her buttock, she growled, "Not again."

Night slammed her into instant sleep.

Chapter Seven

How did I get into so much trouble? And so quick?

Dmitri scrubbed a hand through his hair, the only evident outward display he'd allow at how things had gone from interesting to what-the-fuck in a matter of two days.

Take now for instance. He was a married man—and yes, this marriage was valid, especially once he bedded his new wife. Married and yet his welcome to Teena's family currently involved evading a psychotic father-in-law. Peter wasn't the only one he needed to avoid. Add in dodging the numerous eyes and ears belonging to the lion prides. Even if Arik's pride resided half a country away, there was no doubt that Arik would have some kind of spy network or friendly treaties with the locals to keep watch for a Russian diplomat. Watch and yet not detain.

They couldn't technically stop him, not without permission of the high council—whose palms he greased well—but the local lions could delay his departure and search his plane for evidence of a certain female.

Whom they wouldn't find. He'd made sure of that.

As if that weren't enough, Dmitri also remained on the lookout for assassins who might work for Peter. They could be lurking anywhere. He hoped so. He did so enjoy a little sport.

Also of entertainment were the phone calls he

fielded from people looking for Teena.

"Do you have her?" Arik asked without bothering to say hello.

"I did not kidnap her." Dmitri could say it and sound honest. He hadn't. His henchman had, against his last order.

Luna also contacted him and warned, "Don't you dare leave and fly back to Russia where I can't get you."

As soon as that plane is fueled, we are out of here.

"You'd better not marry her and seduce her either."

I never did like taking orders. Giving them though... If he ordered his new wife to kiss him, would she obey, or would she bite?

Shudder. Either option worked.

So, yes, he did the opposite of what they all said, and he didn't regret it once he did. He still couldn't believe his henchman had even managed to pull the kidnapping off.

When he got the phone call the morning after Meena's wedding saying they'd snagged Teena and were driving to Kentucky, where they would wait for him at the airstrip owned by a family friend, Dmitri might have squeaked.

"You were supposed to abort," he hissed into the receiver, hand cupped over it lest someone overhear. He took himself to the small bathroom attached to the room and closed the door before turning on the water. He relaxed a little. "What the fuck?"

"We kind of didn't get that text, boss," Viktor announced, his Russian loud and booming. "So we went ahead with the plan. We got the girl and are now en route to the rendezvous point." Which meant, when the pride inevitably sent someone to search his plane hangared in the nearby city, they would find nothing, and they'd have no reason to hold him.

A brilliant plan, devised of course by him, and yet how he hated it because it added a few complications, such as ruining his intention to woo Teena.

Then again, perhaps she'd see the romance in it. Drugged and kidnapped, taken on a wild romantic adventure. *With me.*

How could she want anything more?

Knowing what he did meant pretending he didn't. The morning proved tense, the breakfast table sluggish as many slept in after the previous night's festivities.

Peter, however, was there, and as soon as his gaze hit Dmitri, his brow knitted in a frown.

Entertainment for breakfast. How kind of his hosts. After layering a plate from the buffet laid out across two tables, Dmitri seated himself across from Peter.

Dmitri waited until the man took a sip of coffee—black of course and he'd wager no sugar—before saying, "Good morning. I'm surprised you slept, given what your daughter was doing last night."

Out spewed the coffee, and over the table Peter lunged, hands reaching for Dmitri's throat. Except Dmitri wasn't there. "Calm yourself. Such a peasant reaction on a truth. What else would Meena and that mangy husband of hers be doing?"

"You didn't lay a hand on my Teena?" Peter swung his legs off the table, scattering dishes so he could hop off and stand.

Dmitri smiled. "A hand? As if one was enough. I used both of them. And my lips. She kisses quite well.

I shall quite—"

As expected, things got kind of physical at that point, but Dmitri made sure to not damage Teena's father—too much. As for his bruised ribs and swollen right eye, those were for show, so the older man didn't feel slighted. He couldn't hide the truth from his inner sense.

Beaten by an elder. His tiger collapsed in a heap and flung its legs in the air.

Was not. He just got lucky.

Lucky, too, was getting tossed from the property before anyone thought to check on Teena, and even if they had, a note had been left, but Dmitri didn't know how long the forgery would stand.

Best to leave while he could, and even then, he didn't make it to the airport before news of Teena's disappearance hit the gossip lines. That, in turn, led to his plane being searched before he arrived.

Let them. They'd find nothing.

But they sure as hell suspected when his plane dropped out of sight for a quick landing, pickup, and takeoff. If he could have flown straight to Russia, then he would have. But even he knew they'd have to land on the West Coast to refuel in order to ensure they'd make the journey.

Now some would probably say, if he knew he was being chased, and if he valued his hide, then all he had to do was give Teena up. Leave her behind and go home.

To that, the man, not the beast, growled, "Hell no."

But escaping with her was only part of the steps to ensure their future. Once he reached his homeland, he'd have only a little time to convince her to keep him before the council became involved. They tended to frown on shifters, even practically royal ones, abducting women.

Apparently it was *so* eighteen hundreds.

Old didn't mean it wasn't efficient. By marrying Teena, he solved a few issues. First, he could tell the council she was his wife, and they'd have a more difficult time forcing him to give her back. Two, their marriage gave her a legitimate case to stay—*even though just being with me should be enough.* And three, in the eyes of the law and anyone watching, *it makes her mine.*

Mine. Touch and die. How cute that his inner tiger lived by grandmother's unofficial motto.

He wondered how many would admire his perfectly executed escape. Teena certainly didn't seem to appreciate it yet. She threatened to scream and to draw attention so…

He plunged a needle in her ass, and promised to, "kiss it better later."

Her wifely reply. "You'll be dead later."

Not the most promising of words, but hey, at least she planned on a later.

Chapter Eight

Here came a sluggish awakening. Again.

Her tongue felt thick in her dry mouth, her eyelids heavy and refusing to open.

"Blerg." She announced her annoyance to the world in a language lost with the passage of time that harkened back to when cavemen ruled. The one-syllable word conveyed numerous things—that she was awake, thirsty, and too lazy to do a damned thing about it.

Thankfully, someone understood cavespeak.

A pair of hands maneuvered her upright and then anchored her in a seated position. Her head lolled onto a broad shoulder. A familiar scent surrounded her.

Dmitri's scent. My husband.

Funny how the more times she thought or said it, the less strange it seemed to become.

"Drink this." A cold glass, the side slick in moisture, was pressed into her hand.

Greedily, she brought the tumbler to her lips. Missed. The rim hit her cheek, but, good news, it only slopped a bit, and the cold splash on her face helped revive her a little.

She cracked an eyelid, readjusted the glass's angle, and tried again.

Success!

Fresh, clean water wetted her mouth. She gulped it, each swallow a refreshing waker-upper. When she'd drained it almost dry, a hand plucked it from her grip.

"Would you like some more?"

"Is it drugged?" she asked, rather dryly.

His tone held humor as he replied, "Kind of late to be asking now. But no. That was water and nothing more."

Feeling herself getting stronger and more alert, she managed to keep both eyes open and kind of peeked around. Not a single thing looked familiar. "Where are we?"

"Does it matter?"

Of course it did. She needed to escape. Needed to get away from this psycho who'd drugged her and made her his bride.

Why must we leave?

Her lioness honestly wanted to know why she felt a desperate need to flee.

Because. It was the smart thing to do.

But why? Her inner feline truly didn't understand her problem because, technically, Dmitri hadn't done anything to harm Teena. On the contrary, he'd shown an ardent interest in her, enough that he'd taken a page from the romance novels he read, abducted her, and married her.

Which meant he'd now expect to bed her.

The flutter in her belly had nothing to do with fear.

Did he sense the swirl of anticipation that hardened her nipples? Was that why he stiffened beside her? She pushed away from his arms and stood, needing to put a bit of distance between them. Being so close to him muddled her thoughts.

She wobbled but slapped away his hand when he reached out to her.

Don't let him touch me. She found it harder to

think when he was so near.

For distraction, Teena took stock of her surroundings, her very rich surroundings.

Sumptuous didn't begin to describe the room. Imagine a cavernous space with a tall, very tall ceiling, the crown molding on it thick and ornate, which matched the rest of the room. Walls, patterned with paper in subtle gray and silver, were offset by the cream-colored wainscoting hugging the bottom half. Dark wood floors gleamed, their expanse broken only by the furniture that graced the space. Plush carpeting, with intricate designs, defined the areas of the room. A wall of windows overlooked a city, but a city unlike any she'd ever seen.

A city with rooftops dusted in snow.

I don't think I'm home anymore.

The realization should have shocked her, and it did, but more with excitement. For the first time, Teena lived a true adventure, and she was the heroine, not the clumsy instigator.

Legs still wobbly, but unwilling to take the spot beside Dmitri on the sofa, Teena seated herself on a plush dining chair, the back and seat covered in a shark-gray velvet fabric, the table before her a gleaming mahogany inlaid with lighter strips of something more exotic.

Her finger idly traced the design as she sought to compose her thoughts.

"Do you wish stronger refreshment?"

Dmitri's accented words never failed to tickle her, and yet she retained enough wits to reply. "The last time I drank with you, I ended up drugged, brought to a strange location, and married."

"Years from now, you will cherish my romantic gesture."

"Cherish?" She couldn't help a snort. "You'll be lucky if you get to live once my dad finds out."

Poor Daddy. He did his best to abide by the laws, and yet, forensic evidence worked against him. He did get lucky in that key facts tended to get omitted in final reports, leading to him not having as many convictions as expected. Still, though, those couple of years he'd spent in jail during her toddler years had proved rough for their mother. Especially once Teena and Meena learned how to escape their nursery.

"You do realize that the mention of possible pursuit and energetic sport is a positive in my world?"

"Just my luck, I'm stuck with a guy who might be distantly related to my crazy and violent family."

"Fear not, little kitten. We share no common descendants. My grandmother checked."

"When did she have time? We just met." Given he wouldn't meet her gaze, she didn't have to guess. "It wasn't me you checked, of course, but my sister. The one you meant to marry." She couldn't help the flatness of her response.

Despite their absolute devotion to each other, Teena and Meena had enjoyed a certain rivalry of sorts growing up. Meena got an A in math. Teena got one in science. So Meena then went and made the boys' hockey team. She was a damned good player, too, until she got boobs and she declared they got in the way of her stick.

When it came to boys, their tastes varied, as did their expectations from men. Meena just wanted a good time with someone who could handle her two left feet, violent outbursts and all.

As for Teena...*I just want someone to want me.* Her. As she was. Not as second best.

Despite his claim of a romantic gesture, Dmitri

hadn't abducted or married her out of love but because he hadn't married her sister first. Teena had too much pride to accept being a replacement.

Dmitri tilted her chin with a finger, raising her gaze to meet his. "Why are you appearing so sad? Surely you are not upset still at my tiny mistake."

"Tiny? The only reason you're not married to my sister is because she escaped."

"Escaped? Or was she freed by fate because it wanted to help me right a wrong?"

A derisive noise escaped her. "My daddy would say you are so full of poop right now your eyes are brown."

"Your daddy says poop?"

"Of course he does, because the other word is vulgar, don't you fucking know." She deepened her voice in her best imitation of her father.

Dmitri slapped the table as he barked with laughter. "Little kitten, you are just full of surprises."

"I am, and you might not like some of them." Most people tended to mock her once they discovered her biggest weakness. Only Daddy never teased her.

But Dmitri wasn't her daddy. Not even close. He made her think of all kinds of things, none of them decent—but definitely exciting.

"We all have our quirks," he said.

Quirks? Such as her ability to cause trouble simply by entering the room?

No one could ever discover a plausible explanation that day for the dance floor studio flooding, a good thing or Daddy might have had to rob a bank again to find the money to fix it. It wasn't as if she'd done it on purpose. She'd simply bumped that pipe with her head when she bent down to tie her shoe. Not even that hard. Next thing she knew, a hairline crack appeared and moisture beaded. No big deal, right?

When the wave of water rolled from the door in a slow spread of liquid determined to conquer, she'd wisely screamed like everyone else in her dance class and hustled her tutu-ed butt out of there.

However, Dmitri didn't know about these incidents, or the fact that no insurance company would provide coverage to her immediate family anymore. Or that Daddy had bad-ass connections. Her father might call his dealings with less than savory types 'delegation' in front of her sister and mother, but she'd overhead him tell the guys that his staff saved him from doing time, which, in turn, meant spending more time with the family.

Daddy always did put them first.

"I don't understand why you did all this. Are you mentally deranged?" Not that she'd hold it against him. Her family had its fair share of *special* people. "I mean, really, could you have chosen a worse time to kidnap me?" Especially considering he was vastly outnumbered if caught. Then again, it would have taken only one outraged father to end his wedding plans.

"Have you already forgotten the whole thrives-on-danger thing?" Any other male might have looked arrogant rolling his eyes and making that claim. Not so with Dmitri. He managed a subtle wink that just made him appear even more rakish. Dangerous. Probably violent. All things she tried to escape…but kept finding her.

"Fine. You liked the danger of stealing me from under my family's noses. But drugs? Really?" The idea of being incapacitated freaked her out. During that vulnerable state, anything could have happened.

Such as someone changing her out of her dress from the wedding. She peeked down at the track pants and sweatshirt she wore, her feet shod in socks and white sneakers. All of it a perfect fit and definitely not seductress material.

"Who dressed me?" Had Dmitri peeled her gown from her, his hands manipulating her body as he eased the fabric off? Even more important, had he liked what he saw?

She couldn't help a shiver as she wondered if he'd touched, even inadvertently, the swell of her breasts as he clothed her in a track suit. *How sexy. Serviceable cotton athletic wear for my wedding day.* How her mother would cry when she heard. But hey, on the upside, Teena was married. Maybe. "I don't think a marriage is binding if one of us is drugged."

"Only if someone makes complaint. No one would dare."

She waved a hand in the air. "Think again, big guy. I might. I was, after all, the one drugged."

Funny how he just refused to look repentant, he didn't even get close, not with that cat-that-ate-the-canary grin, in this case a canary called Teena.

"You won't turn me in."

"I should just to wipe that smirk off your face," she grumbled. "That wasn't cool, at all."

"The drugs were a regrettable choice. I had hoped to actually woo you into accepting my courtship. However, time was of essence. Hence why you found yourself incapacitated so that my men could spirit you from the ranch."

"Why not wait until I'd left and then nab me?"

"Wait? I don't wait, especially since a delay might have meant another could sweep in to steal you."

She couldn't help but snort. "Because I'm in

such high demand."

"Such perfection as you possess is a treasure many would covet."

The beautiful words affected her more than she liked, but they also reminded her that they were probably spoken to her sister first.

And yet it's not my sister who is now married to him. I am. He's my husband. Mine.

Did it truly matter that he'd not chosen her first? He'd still gone through the trouble to claim her, at least in human legal terms. When it came to the more primal claim, he'd yet to make his mark.

Then again, they'd just gotten married, which made this their wedding night.

Tonight, they'd go to bed together.

Together, which meant sex.

With him.

Gulp.

How terrifying and, at the same time, exciting. Now if she only knew what to do. How did one act when confronted with a new husband? She certainly didn't remember any chapters in her book of manners that her mother made her study that detailed what to do on her wedding night.

Such a heavy and handy tome. It had not only taught her the rules of a lady. It had also given her great posture after the hours she spent with it balancing on her head. Only once did the somewhat unwieldy book take a tumble and break her big toe. But cousin Polly, who'd pushed her, suffered a crooked nose and three loose teeth once Meena was done with her.

Who cared about her traumatic childhood, for others, not her? The more Teena strived to help, the more apologies were necessary.

She might have to apologize tonight to Dmitri

as he discovered another of her quirks. Inexperience.

And no, she was too embarrassed to explain how a girl her age was still a virgin.

He, on the other hand, obviously knew his way around a woman. The thought caused a twinge of jealousy, a twinge that made her understand why her sister reacted so violently with those who touched her Leo.

No one touches what is ours.

Dmitri, though, he could touch her all he wanted.

Anywhere...

Hold on. Stop right there. Had she lost her mind? She barely knew him. How could she think of letting him touch her, and so intimately?

He's a stranger.

Yet so decadently, exotically sexy.

A male who drew her.

My husband.

Hers to touch. Kiss. Love if she so chose.

She could also make him love her.

Make him mine, all mine.

What a delightful concept. Except he didn't seem keen on the whole claiming part, given he stood across the room pouring himself a beverage from a crystal-faceted decanter.

With her hands clasped in her lap, she asked the question burning inside her. "What happens now?" Would he ravish her as the next step in his ploy to reenact the romances he emulated. Should she splay herself on a couch in a pose of acceptance?

Lifting his glass, he swirled the contents before taking a sip. "In about fifteen minutes, we will leave for the airstrip. We will fly to my home in Russia. Your home now as well. But first, we must ensure your family"—his lips twisted—"does not follow. I should hate to have to kill them, especially as they would only be acting in your defense."

"You'd kill them?" she squeaked.

He rolled his eyes. "Well of course I would if they tried to take you from me. You are mine now."

The shiver that went through her had nothing to do with the ominous lowering of his voice as he claimed her, but more with excitement.

How decadent and sexy it sounded when he said it. But still… "I wouldn't like it if you killed my family."

"Then you will do your best to assure them that you are all right." How easily said.

Not so easily done. "What am I supposed to tell them? They'll never believe me if I said I was so enamored of you we eloped."

"And are you?" He fixed her with his mesmerizing gaze.

"Am I what?"

"Enamored of me?" He asked it in a teasing tone, yet was it her, or was there a serious undercurrent within his query?

Surely not. He hadn't married her because of some truly ardent need and desire for her. He merely wished to claim ownership of her genes—and use her wide hips.

Yet, despite his initial reasons, the end result remained the same. *He's mine as much as I am his.*

The very concept thrilled. However, she could almost hear Luna screech, "Stockholm syndrome!"

But was he truly her captor?

He was definitely impatient, or so she gathered, given his actions. However, other than marrying her before she could realize what had happened, and a sedative so she wouldn't get him killed, he'd done nothing more dangerous than give her that wicked smile of his.

Well, he did kiss me.

That probably counted as dangerous, but in a way she wanted more of.

As to him posing another threat... No manacles tethered her in place. No guards held weapons trained on her.

But I'll bet if I try to walk out the door, he stops me.

The electric thrill almost made her try.

A phone waggled in front of her. Her phone, as a matter of fact, which showed a plethora of missed calls and messages when she logged in.

Oh-no.

"How long was I out?" she asked, thumbing through the texts.

"Almost an entire day."

"A day!"

"I needed time to alibi myself as well as secret you away."

"How did you do that? I mean surely someone saw you lugging my unconscious body." Because the last thing she remembered was being in his arms, engaged in a torrid embrace.

Judging by the sudden flare of his nostrils and the smoldering interest in his eyes, he remembered too. "Being a man of vast intelligence—"

Surely she didn't snicker aloud?

"—I ensured my alibi. The wedding was too public to do something. I called over your cousins to take care of you when the drugs took effect. I made sure they saw me go to my room. Your cousin Luna even spent the night in front of my door."

Dear cousin Luna, who brought new meaning

to the word tenacity. Mother suspected a hint of stubborn mule on that side, and Luna's mom, a bold Texan, never denied it.

"So if you were blocked, how did you do it?" How had he managed to secret her away and make her his bride?

"Delegation of course. I am a lord in Russia. I have minions to manage tasks."

She tried not to giggle at the word minions. She did so like the yellow version of them in those movies. Did that make Dmitri, then, the super villain—with the heart of gold?

"Are these minions the same goons Meena was telling me about? I'm surprised you let those bumbling idiots anywhere near me."

Dmitri grumbled. "I'll admit they were not my first choice. My regular left- and right-hand were taken ill. Food poisoning apparently. So I was stuck with Gregori and Viktor. They make better pilots than henchmen."

"You do know the term henchmen makes it sound like you're a bad guy."

"Excellent." He beamed. "One has to make sure to keep one's reputation intact."

"So it's true then? You're a mob lord in Russia?"

"You make it sound so dirty. While my thoughts are dirty, my job is anything but. In the olden days, my role would have been *knyaz* or a *boyar.*"

"What, not a czar? Wasn't that the emperor?" She couldn't help a smirk as she teased him, his ego truly astounding and yet, at the same time, oddly adorable.

"I know my ancestors often strove for such a position of importance. However, I'd prefer to live well into my old age. I get enough assassination attempts with my position as it is."

"And what is it that you do?"

"I am what you Americans would call the alpha of my clan."

"There's got to be more to it than that."

His lips spread in a white grin that held more boyish wickedness than a man of his looks should ever use. "Imports, exports."

"Of?" she prodded.

"Anything that will make money, or give me more power. I control a good portion of the black market."

"So you're a real criminal," she stated.

"In Russia, the proper term is Capitalist, which I assure you is considered more revolting than a thief. Especially since I wear a suit."

"Is it dangerous?"

"Any worthwhile occupation for a male contains elements of danger. It is what we are bred for."

"What of women? How are they treated?" She knew enough about the world to know that different parts of the world meant differences. How would Dmitri treat her? He tended to lean toward the autocratic.

"Women are to be cherished."

Cherished as in restricted from doing things? That didn't sit well if that was the case. "In other words, you think women can't take care of themselves."

Both his brows shot high. "Perish the thought. Women are what keep families from splintering."

"So now you're saying women control stuff? But what about the whole I am alpha, I'm the boss spiel?"

"I am, and I also know when to take advice. Only a stupid man challenges the ideas of an intelligent woman."

"Mama's boy." She coughed it.

He should have taken offense. He smiled. "Perhaps, and yet there is no shame in admitting my mother is an intelligent woman, with a slightly overly enthusiastic response to some situations. But fear not, I'm sure she won't do anything to you. You are, after all, my wife."

"This is priceless. My dad is going to want to kill you and your mother might take an issue with me. So where do we hold family gatherings that have floors that are easy to mop?"

"Here of course. Our floors have centuries of history spilled into them. And a little is more or less expected over here. It's—"

"The Russian way. So you keep repeating." She rolled her eyes but smiled. His matter-of-fact arrogance was natural, not feigned, and totally endearing.

"See, you keep showing your utter perfection by understanding me so well already. My mother will surely recognize this. And if not, fear not, I will protect you."

Her lips pursed. "It seems like our families have some things in common." Her dad went cuckoo over family matters too. A good thing the national park was close to their house and possessed a deep ravine. Otherwise, they might have never gotten to hug their daddy growing up.

She tried to bring their conversation back on track. "We seem to have wandered. So you drugged me, then had your goons somehow kidnap me."

"It took many rubles to convince them to dress

as women, and Viktor has asked for a bonus since a male guest took certain liberties with his person."

Men dressed as women? A certain pair of ugly cousins and the Jell-O shots they pushed on her made her grimace. *I walked right into it.* Not a hint of warning, even from her inner feline.

No need to tell her to hang her head. Someone was feeling embarrassed.

"If you had henchmen doing everything, then what were you doing? Yapping on your phone nefariously plotting?"

"While twisting my imaginary mustache and laughing evilly?" He snorted. "Not quite, little kitten. Given I didn't know how this attempt would go, I elected to rejuvenate myself."

'You slept?"

"Yes. I do not know why you sound so offended. You slept too."

"Because I was drugged."

"Think of it as synchronizing our schedules. I know my brilliant wisdom is sometimes hard to follow, but you'll get used to it."

"I will?"

He smiled with utmost confidence. "Yes. But you are distracting me. You wanted the whole tale. My men drove you to a prearranged airstrip, where they smuggled you aboard my jet within a crate packed amidst some oranges." Which explained the citrus scent that clung to her.

"Where you with them?"

"I wish." He made a face. "Unfortunately, I had to delay my departure from the ranch, lest I draw suspicion. You should be commiserating with me."

"Why?"

"I had to put up with your family at breakfast."

How aggrieved he sounded. "Your disappearance was noted, and can you believe they accused me?" The affront in his tone was genuine.

"But you did it."

"Well, yes, I did, however, the nerve. Accusing a guest at their breakfast table."

"Let me guess. Daddy attacked you."

"We might have exchanged some physical words. Given my treatment, I took my leave and boarded my private jet. We picked you up then flew to the coast. During that flight, I planned our wedding, arranging for a clergy-minded friend of the family to perform the ceremony. As to the rest of our incredible and, yes, you can say it, romantic tale, you know what happened next."

"Yeah, you drugged me and brought me…" She peeked around. "I still don't know where we are."

"Moscow, little kitten, but we shall not be here for long. I popped us into this suite by the airstrip while they refuel and file my flight plan. I'd hoped you'd wake before now."

"Why?"

"So we could consummate our commitment to each other." Said with a completely straight face.

I am married to a whackjob. A cute one, but still… "You are utterly mad. We aren't consummating anything. Maybe in your world, this is romantic, but in mine, this gets you arrested." Which, damn him, was actually kind of romantic. Yet it still begged a question. "I'm still not clear why you'd go through this much trouble. Wouldn't it have been easier to maybe ask me out on a few dates, charm me with your personality, and then pop the question?"

"Dating takes too much time. I wanted you. I took you. You're mine."

She shivered. Women's lib could say what it wanted. Being claimed by a sexy male still held loads of seductive charm.

"What about letting me make that decision?"

The smile he unleashed on her should have come with a warning label—bad decision-making ahead. "You won't regret it, little kitten."

A part of her hoped so, but truly, only time would tell.

The phone in her hand vibrated, shaking with the fury of the incoming call. It didn't take the 'Imperial March' from *Star Wars* belting out for her to guess it was from her father. This would prove interesting.

She waited for Dmitri to snatch the phone from her hand. No way would he let her talk to her dad.

With a nonchalant wave in her direction, he said, "You should answer that. He's very worried."

"What, no warning to say nothing or else?"

"The choice is yours, little kitten. An adventure rife with pleasure, passion, and me. Or my sudden death and a return to your boring life of before. Our future resides in your hands."

She knew what her hands would rather have a hold of. Not the best thought to have when about to deal with the devil that loved her. Taking a deep breath first, she answered. "Hello, Daddy." And yes, she did use her most guileless, little girl voice.

"Don't hello me. Where the fuck are you? I know something's happened. I fucking knew I should have killed that goddamn prick when I first saw him eyeballing you like a piece of bloody steak."

"Daddy. Language!" She mimicked her mother's pitch perfectly.

"Don't you pull that with me! I'll say whatever I goddamn please when my baby girl goes missing."

"I'm hardly missing. I know exactly where I am. I'm here, talking to you right now."

She could almost see the steam blowing out her father's ears. "Don't you pull that semantic shit with me. You know I hate it when your mother does it."

She grinned. He did, which was why her mother kept doing it. Miss Manners 101—cater to your man but always keep him guessing. "Is there any reason why there's like a zillion calls and messages to my phone?"

"You can't just vanish in the night with all your shit and not expect us to get worried. If that Russian prick has you…" He trailed off ominously.

She stood and walked away with her phone pressed to her ear, doing her best to ignore Dmitri as he paced her.

Despite Dmitri affecting a feigned nonchalance, the predator in her could sense the tension coiled in him. If she had to guess, she'd wager if she said the wrong thing he'd lunge to steal back her phone.

Two words. Two words was all it would take to have Daddy and all of the prides he was affiliated with on a plane to Moscow to get her back.

Two words such as 'save me'.

Two words to change the course of her future.

"I'm fine. Super fine as a matter of fact, especially since I escaped before disaster really struck. You know what happens when Meena and I stay in one place too long together." There was a reason their father had learned carpentry, plumbing, and electrical wiring as they grew up. It was cheaper than keeping a handyman on retainer. "Besides, before Meena's surprise wedding, I already had plans to meet friends in

New York. We're going to do some shopping."

"You left without a word to go shopping?" The doubtful tone in her father's voice almost made her laugh.

"Prada's got their new line of purses coming out, and I've been saving."

"You worried us for a purse?"

"Not just any purse. A Prada, Daddy. Mother would understand." When in doubt, toss her mother at him. For some reason, he never argued with her.

"You're sure you're okay?" Aha, there was the crack of doubt she'd chiseled.

"Never better." She met Dmitri's gaze as she uttered the claim, and oddly enough, she meant it.

Forget trepidation or anxiety over what the tiger wanted from her.

Excitement coursed through her veins. Anticipation awakened her senses.

She assured her father a few half-dozen more times she was fine before she finally managed to hang up.

During it all, Dmitri played silent spectator. Then again, why speak when he practically undressed her with his eyes and then visually stroked every inch of her body?

It was more than a girl could handle, and there was nothing technically stopping her from indulging. Women had sex all the time. Casual sex even. She'd held back for so long. She'd held on to an ideal that might never happen.

So what if he doesn't love me yet? We are married. He's mine. She had the choice if she wanted to make this marriage real. To have him in her life, in her bed, and in her heart.

What about inside me?

Desire made her bold.

Tossing the phone to the side, she flung herself on the couch, spread her arms wide, and exclaimed, "Take me. I'm yours."

It might have proven sexier if the French provincial sofa, with its carved spindle legs, hadn't collapsed on the floor.

Chapter Nine

Any other man might have dove on the offering. His little kitten surely tempted with her hair in disarray, her chignon, with all the abuse it had taken, a mess. She wasn't exactly attired in siren clothing, given he'd had her dressed—by a female staff member of the hotel—into something more covering and practical than her wedding apparel. However, the baggy athletic pants and sweatshirt, while not sexy, did not detract from her loveliness.

And she invited him with arms and eyes wide open, ignoring the fact the couch tilted as the broken side sat on the floor.

She wanted him. So why did he hesitate?

"Are you trying to get me close so you can attempt injury to my organs?" His sister enjoyed using that ploy and then taunted him with dire threats that if he told their mother it would prove he was a pussy.

Siblings sucked.

Teena shook her head. "I wouldn't do that."

"Are you hoping to knock me unconscious so you can flee?"

"Somehow I doubt I have anything solid enough to manage that."

True, he did have a hard head.

"Then what is your angle?" Other than the angle she currently splayed in, tilted head down, torso in an odd slump. It was strangely adorable.

"I just wanted to cuddle. No big deal. We are

married, right?" She kind of shrugged. At least she rolled her shoulders, which caused her to slip off the slanted cushions and hit the floor. But she recovered quickly and sat with one leg extended, the other bent, as she leaned back on her arms, thrusting her chest out enticingly.

Cats ever did have a wondrous ability to make even the clumsiest gesture appear as if intentional.

"Yes, we're married."

"Exactly, which means we should consummate this sucker. Usually that requires two of us, in close proximity."

Dmitri frowned. "Aren't you going to argue?"

"Would it matter?"

"Well, no, but still, you must be angry." He'd grown up surrounded by women who didn't need much to let their temper loose.

"Angry that you married me? Not really. And trust me, that surprises me as much as you."

She spoke the truth. He didn't detect any irritation on her part, and that made no sense. Any other woman would have been throwing stuff at him by now and yelling. It was why he glued most things of value down or locked them up. Of course, seeing a priceless vase coming at him, the small table it sat glued on soaring as well, wasn't necessarily an improvement.

He decided to test the waters by truly pointing out why she should be trying to choke him with his own tie. "So you're not miffed at all that I kidnapped you and married you?"

She shook her head.

Why am I hesitating? Didn't I ask for a docile mate? Here she was, ready and willing, except he wasn't.

How the hell did that work?

He headed back for the decanter of brandy.

Funny how his refusal seemed to spark some anger.

"What are you doing? Shouldn't we be getting to the whole honeymoon part?" she demanded.

He almost dropped the bottle he was pouring. "Our flight leaves shortly. I have a car coming to pick us up in less than fifteen minutes."

"That's more than enough time. I think."

He whirled to face her and wondered at her pensive mien. "You think? How long do your lovers usually take?" And could he have their names that he might hunt them down and eradicate them for having touched her first?

"I wouldn't know about length. I'm still a virgin."

The gulp of alcohol hit him wrong, and he sputtered. Choked. He also gasped. She came to his rescue, pounding on his back with vigor.

When he could manage to siphon a small ounce of air, he asked, in a hoarse voice, "What did you say?" Surely he'd misunderstood.

"I said I was a virgin. But not for long. I'm sure you know how to take care of that."

Indeed he did. Or would, if he could gather his senses.

When he'd asked for innocence, he'd never expected true innocence. Not in one as splendid as her.

Pure and mine. Surely there was a catch? "You want me to seduce you?"

"You are my husband. Seduction, claiming, whatever you want to call it. I've been waiting a long time. I can't wait to see what it's like." She smiled at him, expectation thick in the air around her.

Expectations of him.

Was it him, or had this marriage just taken a

troublesome turn? No more was this just a simple joining of bodies. The act of their joining was now fraught with peril. So much pressure now resided on him. A woman's first time was something she never forgot and, from what he'd heard over the years, not always fondly remembered.

What if she hates it?

His sister had once said something about the deed never being able to live up to the expectation.

What if I fail and she never craves my touch again?

Unacceptable.

Teena's first time had to be perfect. Utterly memorable.

With him.

He needed more alcohol.

Even though he faced away from her, she drew near, her hand upon his back in a gesture of consolation. "I seem to have upset you. I'm sorry for being a virgin. I didn't do it on purpose."

She is sorry for being pure? He almost choked again. Slamming the glass down, he whirled to face her. He got sucked in by those beguiling eyes, taken down by the mesmerizing gaze and virgin body of his wife. He wanted to roar and whimper at the same time. "I find your status incredibly attractive."

"Why do I sense a but coming?"

"But I am now perhaps wondering if my hasty actions were wrong. A woman such as you deserves a proper wooing. A perfect seduction. And thus, you shall have it," he resolved in that moment in a stroke of genius to give him time.

His announcement brought a puzzled crease to her brow. "I don't think I understand."

"As you've noted, we are married, and while it is my husbandly right to partake of the carnal pleasures this legal bond brings, I shall abstain and give you the proper wooing you deserve." He'd flirt and tease and tempt her until she begged for him to take her. Then, and only then, would he dare breach her while she was at the height of passion.

"Let me get this straight. You kidnap me and, while I'm still under the influence of drugs, have me hitched to you so you can claim me, but because I'm a virgin, you're not going to sleep with me."

How he loved her quick wit. "Exactly." He beamed at her.

She, on the other hand, sighed and muttered, "Well, isn't that just like my luck to screw me once again?"

Displeasure marked her words, yet that was all she did. She didn't argue. Or throw things. Nor did she try to escape.

She sat back on the couch, the unbroken side, which, as if to taunt her, also collapsed. But Teena didn't flinch, just tucked her legs on the now even sofa.

The spot beside her called. Hell, everything about her called to him.

But no, he didn't trust himself to get that close, despite her seeming distress. Proximity would lead to kissing. Kissing would lead to touching. Touching would lead to him taking her like an animal on the cramped furniture, and he would ruin her first time. Ruin their future sex life.

No. He'd wait. The only problem with waiting was it hurt—and turned a certain part of his body blue. But at least he respected his new bride.

A shame she didn't appreciate it.

Chapter Ten

Just what does a virgin wife have to do to get debauched?

Teena really wanted to know. Offering herself hadn't worked. Telling her husband he would be her one and only seemed to set off a state of panic. Would she have to tie Dmitri down and have her way with him?

The idea had merit, if she had the guts to go through with it, but she didn't. Only too easily she could imagine the disaster if she went that route. The use of ropes, or even a belt, might result in a loss of circulation to his limbs. Throwing herself at him could result in bodily harm.

Daddy might be able to handle his baby girl, but other men tended to get squashed. Not that Teena knew this first-hand, but she'd heard enough stories from her sister, Meena, and helped her send enough "Hope that broken collarbone mends soon," cards to know it happened.

If Teena had the guts, she would have stripped, right down to her birthday suit.

Resist that!

However, shyness wouldn't let her.

It seemed, even married, she was doomed to fail with men. One man. Her husband. *My mate.*

Despite his initial attempt to marry her sister, Teena had now spent enough time with him to come to one certainty. Dmitri was hers.

As in her soul mate. Her one and only. Her

man.

Now if only the brash Russian she'd met would make her certainty a reality instead of putting her off with a misguided notion that she needed wooing.

The limo ride to the airport was a quiet one. She sat across from him, watching as he made calls, speaking in Russian, the rolling cadence of the foreign words a sensual delight. Was he the type to purr Russian endearments in her ear? Maybe one day she'd find out.

When he hung up, she asked, "That sounded pretty serious. Problems?"

"Nothing unusual. Just my sister and mother, being brought up to speed on our current situation."

"Are they upset that you married me without them there?"

"I am their lord. It does not matter."

She arched a brow at his arrogant statement.

He laughed. "Okay, I heard a long spiel about how I was an ungrateful son robbing a mother of her chance to throw a lavish wedding and show those other clan upstarts how royalty weds. Whereas, my sister said I was a boorish ass who needed to get clubbed over the head for acting like a Neanderthal."

She couldn't help a smile. Despite his complaints, she could hear the fondness in his voice. "You sound close to your family. Do you live with them?"

A grimace twisted his lips. "Yes. But I assure you my home is quite large. While they are situated in the east wing, we have the entire west wing to ourselves."

"Wings? Just how large is this place?"

He gave a negligent wave of his hand. "The size doesn't matter."

The imp in her, the one that had obviously heard her sister one too many times, retorted, "Funny, I was always told by the girls that it's all about the size. The bigger, the better."

While her own words didn't make her blush, his reply did. "I assure you, I have more than enough size to please you, little kitten. And my oral skills are to scream for."

The ardent flare in his eyes stole her breath, and she thought, for a moment, he would lunge from his seat and join her, maybe kiss her, except his damned phone rang and broke the spell.

Arriving at the airport, they went through a prioritized screening routine, which involved very little checking but a whole bunch of handshaking.

"How did you manage that?" she asked as they exited the main building and headed toward a small plane sitting outside a hangar.

"Manage what?"

"Getting me out of the United States, past all the security clearances. I'd heard they'd cracked down on travelers."

"I have connections, little kitten. And when those fail, a little bit of money helps ease the way."

How ironic that she, the one who strove the hardest to follow the rules, ended up married to the guy determined to break all of them.

He's the complete opposite of me.

Perhaps she was being stupid. How would this work? Did this crazy marriage stand a chance?

Yes.

It took her inner feline to remind her that her prim and proper mother was happily married to their less-than-law-abiding dad.

The question was, would they end up being as

in love as her parents?

Time would tell. Or Daddy would kill him.

Aboard Dmitri's private jet, Teena lounged on a creamy soft leather seat while watching Dmitri tap away at his tablet, his brows drawn together in a frown. Tension rolled from him.

"Is something wrong?" she asked. Had his mother expressed her unhappiness some more in written words?

"Two more in my clan have gone missing. That makes five in as many months."

"Did they move away?" It wasn't uncommon for grown shifters to change places. It made the prospect of finding a suitable mate more likely.

"No, they didn't move. One left behind a pregnant wife while the other was engaged to be married. They seem to have disappeared without taking anything with them, not even their identity cards or any belongings."

She joined him in frowning. "That is odd. Do you have enemies? Could they have perhaps taken them in order to try and manipulate you?"

He snorted. "Of course I have enemies. I would not be a proper leader if I did not have any. Yet, usually feints at my power come with taunts and the identity of the responsible party for glory."

It was scary enough that she was leaving her world and family behind, but the idea she might walk into danger caused a momentary flutter. "Are we in danger?"

"I will not let you come to harm." Spoken with the utmost confidence.

She believed him, which was what gave her the boldness to move from the chair to his side then his lap.

To his credit, he didn't gasp when she dropped in his lap—and nothing cracked—but he did sound wary when he asked, "What are you doing?"

Doing what she'd observed her mother do when she wanted something from her father. Then again, given how many times she'd observed her parents disappear behind their solid oak door, her mother had never had to work this hard at seduction.

Teena draped her arms around his neck and leaned in close. The plane lurched as it rolled in to motion.

Bonk.

She rubbed her noggin. "Sorry."

"No need to apologize, little kitten. Accidents happen."

"More often than you can imagine," was her dry retort.

Now seated in his lap, she found herself at a loss. He'd yet to dump her on her butt, but he'd also not done anything other than loosely hold her either.

Did he welcome her advance? Had she proved too forward?"

He stroked a strand of her hair, tucking it behind her ear. "You are nervous." Stated, not asked.

"A little nervous."

"Is it the plane? Are you afraid of flying?"

She shook her head.

"Then why the trepidation?"

She wondered if he was being deliberately obtuse. Then again, he had his own way of looking at the world. Perhaps he truly didn't know what had her on edge. "You make me nervous."

"Me?"

She nodded.

Both his brows raised high. "That makes no

sense. You seated yourself on my lap. If my proximity bothers you, then why do that?"

She squirmed, her spot atop his thighs made interesting by the growing bulge under her bottom. At least one question was answered. He did desire her.

"I sat here because I wanted to." She did, but now wondered at her choice. He didn't seem very receptive. Maybe she should move.

His arms closed around her. "I am pleased that you are not frightened by me. Or is this a ploy to get me to relax so you can kill me?"

"You have a really suspicious mind."

"A man in my position always has to wonder at the ulterior motives of others."

"Even your wife's?" she asked.

"Especially those close to me. It is often those you trust most that betray you the worst."

How sad he sounded. "It sounds like you're speaking from experience."

"More like the past. A past long gone. Long forgotten, and nothing to do with our future."

"Our future—Eep." The plane lifted from the ground with a sudden twitch, and gravity sucked at her.

Lucky her, Dmitri was belted in, and even luckier, he held on to her firmly. He laughed. "Fear not, I have you."

Indeed he did, and as their gazes meshed, heat ignited between them. She leaned toward him, and he met her halfway, his lips finding hers for a sensuous embrace. Nibble. Suck. A tender pulling of willing flesh.

He kissed her and tasted her as if she were the most delicious treat ever, his soft sounds of enjoyment making her squirm in his lap.

She let her hands roam his broad shoulders,

trusting him to hold her up, to keep her from falling.

How wide he seemed, the breadth of him absolutely delightful. The ridge of hard muscle met her questing palms as she smoothed them over his upper body, exploring all the parts she could.

When the plane leveled off, he joined the quest, his hands stroking her back, sliding under her shirt, the shock of his fingers dancing on her skin making her breathing hitch.

Oh how she wanted more. The decadent thrust of his tongue into her mouth saw her groaning. How could the sensual slide of their tongues prove so arousing?

The heat between them should have burned their clothes to ashes. She almost wished it would so she could feel his skin. Touch the flesh hidden from her.

Instead, she hit the damned floor as a massive jolt shook the plane, dumping her from his lap.

She might not have glared so hard if his sputtered, "Little kitten, are you all right?" hadn't been followed with laughter.

"Not funny," she grumbled as she stood then stumbled as the plane lurched again.

The intercom on the plane crackled to life. "Please note we are experiencing turbulence. It is recommended you buckle into a seat, as it could get more violent." Said in a voice even more accented than Dmitri's.

Plopping back onto the couch, she located a belt and buckled it. Foiled by bad weather.

But hopeful now.

He wants me. And one thing was for sure. She wanted him too.

Chapter Eleven

Damn how he wanted her.

Now.

Here.

Who cared if there was no bed and their privacy was iffy? His little kitten had made the first move. She had seated herself on him as if she belonged on his lap, which she did.

Despite her innocence, and his methods, she seemed prepared to make the marriage real.

She accepted and wanted him.

Or was this just a ploy?

Suspicion was an ugly beast. It tainted the most innocent of actions with doubt. Dmitri had dealt too many times in his life with people who lied, and lied well. He wanted to believe the guilelessness in her actions and gaze, but what if she fooled him. After all, her twin had been adamantly opposed to them uniting, a good thing too.

He could see now just how wrongly suited they were for one another. But that did not mean Teena felt the same way. Her words and actions seemed to indicate otherwise, or was he letting his own hope and attraction to her cloud his judgment?

I am not wrong.

It just wasn't allowed. If he let doubt seep in now, he'd forever question, and Dmitri wasn't one to live with that kind of uncertainty on his back.

He would trust his little kitten wanted this

marriage to work, especially since, other than a few words—really just a token protest—she had done nothing yet to fight it.

The rumble and toss of the plane as it fought the vicious air currents proved lulling especially since, now in Russian territory, he felt a lot of the tension that had followed him as he escaped from the United States with his prize easing.

He yawned and smiled as he noted Teena trying to hide a jaw-cracking one behind a hand. Perhaps a short nap was in order before they landed and he began the task of wooing his wife.

The popping of his ears woke him. They must have begun their descent, except, when he peered from the window, instead of the familiar farmfields and pathways of roads he expected to see, mountainous terrain and thick forest tops, dusted in white, greeted him.

This isn't right. He'd flown this route too many times to think this was normal. Had his pilot veered off course?

He unbuckled his lap belt and stood as Teena, her voice thick with sleep, asked, "Are we there yet?"

"Soon, little kitten. I must speak with the pilot for a moment. Rest some more."

He let his fingers stroke across her cheek as he passed her, and her lashes fluttered to tickle the tops of her cheeks. She did not flinch from his touch. On the contrary, a small smile curved her lips.

He would have loved to spend a moment with her, especially with her so soft and desirable. However, the sense of something not right nagged him.

Reaching the cockpit door, he pulled the handle, only to find it locked. How odd. Gregori and

Viktor usually never locked it.

A sharp rap on the door yielded no result. A frown knitted his brow, and he banged again.

Still no answer, which didn't bode well.

This is why I hate flying. At least on the ground, he controlled what happened. Up here, he was at the mercy of the pilots.

"Is something wrong?" Teena asked, having come up behind him.

"Wrong? Of course not." He lied with finesse. "Simply an issue with our flight plan, which I plan to resolve shortly."

"Issue? What kind of issue?"

"Merely we are not where we should be. But I am sure there is a good reason for it." And if not, Gregori and Viktor would feel his wrath.

She giggled.

Odd because he'd not meant to make a jest. "What is so funny?"

"Just that wouldn't it be ironic if you kidnapped me, only to end up kidnapped yourself?"

"No one would dare." Not if they wanted to live. But then again, most of his enemies did have a death wish.

He rapped on the door again, and this time, he got an answer. Just not one he liked. "Fuck off, mate. I ain't letting you in."

That wasn't Gregori. Or Viktor. Or anyone who worked for Dmitri. Earlier, when someone had spoken, he'd been distracted and had not questioned the muffled voice. However, now he had to wonder who the hell sat in the cockpit.

"I've been hijacked." The nerve of it stunned for a moment.

"By terrorists?" she asked.

Well, that was jumping to extremes. He quickly set her straight. "Bah. I wouldn't call him that. I'm not terrified, are you?"

She blinked. "You do know the meaning of terrorist, right?"

"Yes. I also know the meaning of corpse, which is a more apt name for the idiot in that cockpit."

"That idiot is flying this plane."

"Which means he's hardly going to do anything to harm us while we're in the air." Yes, once again, his vast intellect located the most pertinent fact.

She jabbed at his fact with a sharper one. "Nope, you're right, which means he's going to take us to somewhere he feels in control before telling us what he wants. I guess we wait and see."

"Wait?" Dmitri scoffed. "Hardly. Have you forgotten? I am not a patient man."

"Except when it comes to deflowering your wife," she grumbled, only a second too late realizing she'd said it aloud. Her cheeks bloomed with color.

"Waiting in this case is good."

"Why, because it makes the heart grow fonder?"

"No, because it makes you more desirous of my touch." At her rounded O of surprise, he winked. "Now, little kitten, I will need you to stand back whilst I pay our misguided pilot a visit."

"How? The door's locked. Do you have a key?"

Probably, but damned if he knew where it was kept. Before he flew again, he'd make sure he kept it on his person. In the meantime, though, he had a door to open.

Teena moved away, giving him ample room. Taking a step back, he lifted a foot and kicked.

Thud. He made an impressive noise, left a bit of

a dent, but the door mocked him by not opening.

Bang. Bang. Bang. Over and over he kicked the damned thing. While stricter aviation safety rules had made the cockpit doors on commercial jet liners virtually impermeable, on smaller private jets, like his Cessna Citation, the door was more to provide privacy to the occupants.

The door caved in, the metal frame holding it bending enough to pop the lock. It took him only a moment to notice that the cockpit held two people. One never even bothered to turn around and look, but he wasn't Dmitri's greatest threat. That was reserved for the guy standing in front of him holding a gun.

His feline proved less than impressed. Bringing a weapon to a shifter fight. Some people had no honor.

"Back up, mate." Words punctuated by a wave of the gun.

Not usually one to obey, Dmitri, for the moment, did as told. It might have had a lot to do with the barrel pointed right at his forehead. While he might heal at a faster rate than a human, a bullet this close would kill him.

Totally unacceptable. I've yet to bed my new wife.

But did this idiot—sniff—who stunk of reptile, give a damn? Apparently not, as he snarled, "Move to the back end of the cabin, or I'll blow your brains out."

A few things happened then. For one, Teena moved, but given she had her wide-eyed gaze trained on the hijacker, she didn't mind where she was stepping.

Her foot caught on the edge of a seat. The plane chose that moment to tremble, the wind buffeting it. It threw his new wife off balance, and she toppled toward the wall of the craft. It also happened to be the wall with the door.

She caught the lever that sealed it shut, and all might have been fine if the gunman hadn't ordered her to, "Stand up and put your hands where I can see them."

The plane still wobbled, so it wasn't by intention—or so Dmitri assumed—that she stood still grasping the lever. It didn't make a sound as it rotated. However, once it reached a certain spot, the sound of the cabin seal being breached proved loud.

The gunman barked, "Get away from the fuckin' door. Now."

And that was when shit got really interesting.

Chapter Twelve

Oops. The suction of air, whistling at the intense pressure, didn't bode well.

Teena stumbled away from the opening in the plane. She'd not meant to open the door. Didn't those things have a better lock?

It didn't really matter now.

When she'd pushed away from the door, just doing as she was told, it swung open, and stayed open, their aerial momentum keeping it from slamming shut. A big, wide hole in the side of the plane that resulted in a certain suction inside the cabin.

Totally unpleasant, but thankfully their heads didn't explode. Luckily Teena knew enough about flying—given the incidents she'd lived through—to know they were low enough and that pressurization of the cabin wasn't necessary. However a pressurized environment sure made for a more pleasant flight, given the open door created a whirlwind within.

Her hair whipped around her head and blinded her. Unable to see, she stumbled away from the deadly opening—big open sky without wings to fly, never a good thing. Just ask Uncle Marty.

She tripped over the couch—damn her clumsy, giant feet—and fell on to it.

While she struggled to get upright, a task made increasingly difficult as the plane wobbled in the air, she noted that Dmitri, rather than retreating from the guy holding the gun, rushed to confront him.

Heroic or stupid?

Either way, she found herself riveted and watched the unfolding action.

Her new husband possessed quick movements. In the blink of an eye, he clasped the wrist holding the weapon and forced it to aim overhead. With his other arm, he hugged the hijacker close in an attempt to choke him.

Channeling her twin, Teena couldn't help but yell, "Get him!"

Dmitri grunted in reply as he and the gunman danced clumsily. Both fought to gain control of the situation, but the tight confines and the rough humping of the plane worked against Dmitri.

I should help. But how?

The gun. If she could get the gun, that would even things out.

Springing to her feet, she held out her arms and bent her knees as she walked up the pitching aisle between the plush seats.

Much like a tossing ship, the plane rolled and dipped. It was enough to make a girl toss her cookies. But given many of the trips Teena had gone on had some kind of issue—like the ferry that hit a sudden storm and took on water or the helicopter that hit a huge pelican and went spinning out of control—she had learned to not lose the contents of her tummy.

Reaching the struggling pair, she had to hop on to a seat as they grunted in her direction. The added height was perfect though, as she could clasp, with both hands, the gun, which the guy released especially once she leaned in and bit a few fingers.

"Bitch!" screamed the bleeding hijacker.

"Don't you call my wife names!" Dmitri bellowed. He pulled back a fist and punched the fellow in the face. Once, twice.

The hijacker reeled, his eyes momentarily unfocused, but when they did blink and regain clarity, he saw her and lunged.

She squeaked, and dodged to the side.

"Aaaaaaaaaaaaaaaah!" The guy's scream receded in volume as he fell from the plane.

Biting her lip, Teena couldn't help but utter, "Oops. I didn't mean for that to happen."

Dmitri beamed. "Beautifully done, little kitten. Now shall we take care of the pilot?"

Except the pilot didn't want taking care of. Emerging from the cockpit, a parachute strapped to his back and goggles hiding his eyes, the second hijacker aimed yet another gun at them.

"Two guns on my plane?" Dmitri exclaimed. "Who the hell has been bribing my officials? This is simply unacceptable."

"Don't come near me," the pilot said as he inched toward the opening.

"I can't let you jump," Dmitri said with a shake of his head. "So get back in there and fly the plane. If you listen now, then maybe I won't kill you later when I question you on who paid you to do this."

"Fuck you." With those words, the pilot dove toward the opening, and Dmitri couldn't move fast enough to stop him.

He muttered an expletive in Russian.

So vulgarly sexy, but not helpful.

"This is not the time to bitch. We have to do something."

Except he didn't move. "Why aren't you panicking?"

She shrugged. "When you've been on a ferry that capsized, on a plane that had its landing gear jam, and a bus whose brakes failed, something like this kind of seems normal. I warned you trouble followed me."

"Whereas, luck loves me. Fear not, little kitten. We shall prevail."

Given his confidence, that could only mean, "You know where to find more parachutes?"

"Nope. The one the pilot wore must have been brought aboard."

They both clued in at the same time, but she said it first. "What about the guy who fell? Maybe he had one."

They both couldn't fit through the doorway at once. Being a lady, she let Dmitri poke around inside. He emerged with a triumphant grin. "Success!" The parachute dangled from his hand.

Perhaps they would survive after all. *There's hope I won't die a virgin yet!*

The straps for the chute required loosening, and she handled one side while he did the other. All the while, the wind whistled through the open door.

Just as he exclaimed, "I think it's loose enough for me to cinch it on," the plane, unmanned and on some kind of autopilot, wobbled hard. Teena stumbled, her arms windmilling, the suction of the door pulling at her.

"Eep!" She couldn't help a squeak of fear.

But Dmitri wasn't about to let her down—especially not thousands of feet down, where a landing would mean a funeral instead of a honeymoon. His hands clasped hers and drew her back to the center of the plane and safety.

He saved me. It was so utterly romantic.

However, in saving her, he'd dropped the parachute on the floor. Teena could have predicted what happened next. The plane decided to tilt again,

and their only hope went sliding out the open door.
Damn it.

Chapter Thirteen

The look of horror on Teena's face almost made Dmitri laugh. However, this wasn't time to indulge in amusement. Later, over some true Russian vodka and in front of a roaring fire, they could laugh about the unlucky chain of events. Then make love.

Rawr.

First, though, survival.

Stepping through the busted door into the cockpit, Dmitri found himself stymied by the myriad dials, buttons, and flashing lights. Why couldn't he spot one that said 'press this to land the freaking plane'? All he wanted to do was fly the damned thing long enough to land it without crashing and bursting into a major ball of flames.

How complicated could it be?

He dropped into a seat and made the mistake of looking out the front window. The plane was well below cloud level and moving fast. They seemed to be heading at a downward angle, and it was a tossup whether they'd hit the ground or the mountain that grew bigger in his sight first.

Challenging odds. Perfect. It would make their escape all the more awesome in the retelling—with him cast in the role of hero, of course.

Face still pale, Teena popped her head into the cockpit and shouted to be heard over the plane and wind noise. "Do you know how to fly this thing?" she asked.

A male never admitted defeat. "More or less. I've watched numerous movies featuring planes."

"Oh god, we're going to die."

"Have a little faith. I wouldn't let my wife die a virgin. Now, I suggest you buckle in. This could get a little bumpy."

With a grumbled, "Why can't traveling ever be easy," she dropped into the seat alongside him and clipped in as he studied the gibberish in front of him.

He couldn't have said what all the damned things meant. Airspeed indicator seemed kind of self explanatory, torque a little less clear, and the dial labeled directional gyro sounded like something he had for lunch once.

"What are you going to do?" she asked, studying him as he studied the console.

"Since there is no time to read an instruction manual, and being a man, we don't believe in following direction anyway, I believe I shall have to wing it." He waited for her to laugh at his pun.

Too subtle? Or too soon? Okay, so perhaps now wasn't the time for levity. The mountain seemed to be winning the race when it came to who-will-we-crash into-first. Time to do something. Anything.

Out of the mess of dials, flashing lights, and buttons, he did recognize one thing—a steering wheel.

His male gene kicked in as he grasped the wheel and the theme for *Top Gun* hummed through his mind. He should note that, when he'd watched it, he rooted for the other side because it drove his sister crazy, especially since she had the biggest crush on Tom Cruise until she found out how old he was in real life.

Given the mountain loomed fast, he yanked hard on the wheel. The plane shuddered, and something metallic screamed as the plane tried to go vertical. Shit. He pushed down on the wheel, too hard again, and Teena let out a yell as they began to plummet, the nose of the plane aiming right for the ground.

Gentle. I must be gentle.

Brute force wasn't the way to fly this thing. Keeping that in mind, he pulled the wheel again, softer this time. At first he wondered if it would work, but gradually, their angle corrected until they were on a somewhat even keel, that wobbled and was still headed straight for a bank of mountains.

"Um, Dmitri."

"I know. I can see them."

Slowly, he pulled down on the wheel, angling their ascent, but the mountain was still fast approaching. He angled some more and felt beads of sweat pop on his forehead.

Him, nervous? Never. Just like he would never admit he held his breath as they just cleared the top of the first ridge.

"Aha. See. Nothing to it."

Before she could reply, the radio crackled. "Head Hunter to Fang. You're coming in low, please advise."

Dmitri looked in vain for a reply button. "How the fuck do I answer?"

"Answer? Are you crazy?"

"Only one sixteenth from my mother's side. Although there apparently might be some psychosis on my father's."

"I was being rhetorical."

"I wasn't. Now where is the communicator? I am in the mood to speak to the person in charge."

"No talking for you. You, my crazy husband, need to concentrate on flying this thing. I will take care of our callers." Teena pulled a receiver on a curly cord from her side of the dashboard. "Head Hunter, this is Peeved Lioness. Fang is indisposed. Over."

Dmitri could have kissed her for not having hysterics. He could have seduced her for being so calm and sexy. He could totally love her for being perfect.

"What happened to Fang? Who is this?"

"This is peeved lioness, and might I add you chose the wrong plane to hijack?"

To add weight to her words, and because it was so much fun, Dmitri held out his hand and asked for a turn. She wasn't the only one who enjoyed meting out a good threat.

She handed him the handset.

Depressing the button on the side, in a low tone—the one his sister called his "Oh shit. Hope your will is in order"—Dmitri said, "I am death. Run. Run fast and far now because I will be coming to kill you."

And then he hung up.

He kind of expected the person to call back, or retort, but the communication line remained clear.

Before he could decide if that was good or bad, Teena said, "Do you think that was wise?"

"It is only fair to warn my prey that I'm coming. At least then it provides a little sport."

"But you don't even know what the guy was guilty of."

"If he was working in cahoots with those who kidnapped us, then he is guilty by association. I do not tolerate threats to me and, most especially not, my wife."

"You and my daddy have a lot in common."

Argh, compared to her father. Just what every potential lover wanted.

About to retort, he bit the words as something

caused the plane to tilt. Then the windshield cracked as something hit it.

"Dammit, someone is firing at us."

Would the trouble plaguing them never end? A man liked a little action and adventure to get the blood flowing, but this was getting beyond ridiculous. How was he supposed to properly woo and bed his new wife if shit kept happening?

More slugs hit them, or so he could only assume as the pitch of the motor changed. A faint whiff of smoke came to him, and the dials on his dash went crazy, spinning, flashing, in general conveying a not-good vibe.

"I think we need to land." She suggested it, and he had to agree.

"Land? No problem. Hold on, little kitten. This might get a little rough."

Chapter Fourteen

Apparently his idea of a little rough and hers weren't the same.

As Dmitri angled the plane downward, the very air seemed to fight them. The craft bucked and wobbled and jerked, but she could handle that motion. It was the visual of the treetops they were heading for, visible even through the spiderwebbed window, that had her gripping her seat tightly.

There was nowhere to land. Trees were everywhere, their tops reaching high and clustered densely. No room for a small plane and its occupants.

But they didn't have a choice. The smell of smoke grew thicker, the whining pitch of the motors almost painful.

The belly of the plane dipped lower, low enough that it scraped the tips of the tallest conifers. Dragged and snapped the tops of more. A good thing she wore a belt because the forest seemed determined to claim them, their speed going from rapid rush to bouncing, jerking, slowing halt.

From side to side, her head snapped, and she couldn't stop a few screams. But screaming was good. It meant she still lived, for the moment.

When they finally came to an abrupt stop, it took her a moment to release her last breath. Was it over? Had they truly survived?

She cracked open an eye and peeked. She noted the appearance of branches outside the window. The trees had cushioned their fall.

"We made it?" She couldn't help the surprised query.

"Of course we did," Dmitri announced with brash assurance. "I told you I'm lucky."

Crack.

"You just had to tempt Murphy didn't you," she grumbled.

"I spit in his face, whoever this Murphy is."

The whole plane shuddered and groaned as it tilted.

Good thing she was still buckled in because the plane now tilted at a very steep angle and faced down.

"Um, Dmitri. How do we get out of this?" she asked, eyeing the mountainside that stretched under them, a snowy slope with lumps of white, heaps of gray, and copses of trees lining it. If she skied she would have loved the pristine trail, but she'd tried that only once. The avalanche was enough to convince her it wasn't her sport.

"I think, little kitten, that perhaps we should try not moving."

"And how will that help?" she asked as the craft creaked and tilted a little more forward.

"It doesn't, but you should use the few seconds we have left to take in a deep breath and hold on tight because I do believe we are in for a ride."

With a groan, the plane pitched farther, and branches cracked. The woods that had initially cushioned their fall and saved them now apparently didn't want them. They were dumped onto the mountainside.

And what did Dmitri advise they do? Forget advice. He yodeled, "Wheee!"

Was that idiot tiger seriously having fun?

"You are crazy!" she yelled as she stared in horror at the rushing landscape.

"Not crazy. Russian." And yes, he smiled as he said it. She saw him because she couldn't help looking at her deranged husband.

Then she kept staring at him because he was much more fun to look at than the direness of their situation as they careened down the mountain at breakneck speed.

Extreme tobogganing, the kind her sister would have totally enjoyed but Teena could have done without. The jaw rattling and jouncing sucked, but the part she worried about most was the stopping.

Would they hit something big enough to halt them? Would they fly off a cliff and then plunge to their deaths, or would they hit the bottom of the incline and coast for a while until they slowed to a stop?

None of the above.

After a wild ride that rattled her brain, the slope evened out, and they shot forward into what seemed like a vast, cleared space. Except it wasn't a snowy clearing. The lake they spun out on formed an almost perfect ice rink, the center of it snow free, as the wind had pushed it against the banks.

The plane came to a screeching stop, and Teena dared to breathe again.

"I don't believe it. We made it. We're alive. We're"—*Crack. Damn you, Murphy*—"fucked!"

Chapter Fifteen

A dirty word from his little kitten's mouth? How utterly decadent, and he might have kissed those dirty, dirty lips if only the situation were a little more promising.

Cats hated water, especially arctic-cold water, which was why Dmitri didn't want to dwell on what would happen if the plane went through the ice. He could see Teena understood the dilemma, but his brave little kitten, other than that vulgar expletive, handled the pressure well.

"I think we should perhaps vacate the plane," he said.

The crack notwithstanding, the smell of smoke hadn't diminished, and where there was smoke, everyone knew there was fire. The heat from a blaze would not aid their situation.

Melted ice was only one of their possible problems. Despite his usual optimism, Dmitri was a touch concerned about what would happen if any flames managed to reach some of the fuel.

Dmitri enjoyed watching fireworks, not becoming part of them.

"Exit the plane? Gee, why didn't I think of that?" she grumbled as she unclipped her belt. She stood then froze as a groan made the plane tremble. "Is this a not-so-subtle way of your country telling me I need to lose weight?"

"Never. You are perfect as you are. However,

you must fish for compliments later, little kitten. I believe speed is called for."

"What about you? Why haven't you unbuckled?"

"Fear not, wife, I shall follow you. But I think it best if we don't apply more weight than needed at one time, as we don't know what part of the plane is most at risk of breaking the ice."

For a moment, she hesitated, peering at the door, the windshield, then him. She took a step toward the door, stopped and whirled, bending to press a quick kiss to his lips.

Then she fled, the lingering warmth of the embrace she gave him making him smile foolishly.

As if to taunt him, the plane shuddered. "Behave," he told it in Russian. "It is not my time to die." Not when he had yet to taste the nubile delights of his wife.

My wife. A woman who had almost died numerous times in the last hour. Nothing said welcome to my homeland like being hijacked, held at gunpoint, almost falling out of a plane, crashing, and then tobogganing onto thin ice. But, on a more positive note, they still lived. They were also far from safe.

Cold seeped, the insidious invisible predator looking to burrow its way into his bones, and if he, a native to this land, felt it, then how much more so his delicate little kitten?

He heard her holler over the dying whir of the motor. "I'm out and heading to shore."

Time for him to execute his escape. He needed to survive if he was to keep Teena alive.

He needed to make it out of here if he was to seek his revenge. Heads would roll.

Playtime, rumbled his tiger.

Later, Dmitri replied, if there was a later. Taking light steps, he eased his bulk through the slanted doorframe and then held his breath as the floor under his feet shifted.

The bright daylight streaming through the opening in the side beckoned. However, out there lay the frigid bitch with her icy fingers who liked to drag the unwary and ill-prepared down into her deadly embrace.

We need more clothes. Which meant he needed to get to their luggage.

Except the rear cargo area no longer existed. At the rear of the plane gaped blue sky. There would be no additional layers for them.

Damn.

Dmitri scanned the interior and spotted his phone on a chair, jammed between the seat and back cushion. He shoved it in a pocket before he lifted the padding to reveal a storage compartment and a pair of neatly folded blankets. He grabbed them and let the lid to the hidden recess slam shut.

Crack. Groan. Shudder.

He'd run out of time. Blankets in hand, he dashed for the back of the plane, mostly because the front end seemed determined to lean forward. Fighting against the increasing incline, he sprinted the last few feet toward the torn opening and leaped.

His legs ran, pumping in mid air, propelling him forward.

Look at me. I'm flyin—

Oomph. He hit the ice and immediately tucked and rolled, a good thing too, as the piece he landed on heaved and broke off. Actually the whole lake seemed determined to splinter into chunks. He could hear the ominous pop as the hairline cracks in the frozen membrane spread, zinging with lightning speed, the cold water looking to swallow the skin covering it and anything else it caught.

It won't catch me.

Dmitri ran as fast as he could, legs pumping and adrenaline coursing. To this point he'd proven lucky, the slight ridges in the ice and excellent balance keeping him from slipping. But as soon as he thought it, his foot finally hit a smooth spot and skewed sideways. It threw off his entire balance.

Lucky him, he didn't crash. A certain kitten grabbed a hold of his waving hand and gave him enough counter weight for him to prevent a head-long crash.

He made it to shore, or at least the thick snowbank. Breathing hard, he took a moment to survey the lake just in time to see the jagged tail end of the plane sink below the surface.

"I think I need to buy a new plane."

"We're stuck in the middle of nowhere, with no clothes, no supplies, nothing, and you're worried about buying a new toy?" Arms hugging herself, his kitten shook, her lips a shade of mauve that did not suit her.

"Wear this." He tossed the blankets around her shoulders, but they weren't enough to fight the chill. He needed to find them shelter and fast.

Clasping her hand in his, he tugged her away from the edge of the water. Out in the open, they were subject to gusty wind. They should head to the shelter of the trees. At least there, he could perhaps build them a fire.

But what of the smoke? Our enemies hunt us.

Excellent point. He'd make a big fire to point the way. He really wanted to talk to whoever shot his plane down. Cessnas weren't cheap.

Teeth chattering, body moving sluggishly, poor Teena did her best to keep up with his longer stride.

Dmitri felt the cold, perhaps not as keenly as her but enough that he knew what had to be done. He stopped even as she continued on a few paces, only brought short by the fact that his hand held hers.

"Wh-wh-at d-d-doing?" she chattered practically incoherently.

"Giving you a peek at the goods," he replied as he stripped off his suit jacket. The tie he loosened and pulled from his neck. He then pulled off his shirt, baring his chest.

"D-d-d-umb."

"Not really. You'll see." He pulled the blanket from her shoulders and then tugged his shirt onto her.

She tried to protest. "No."

He ignored her and layered the coat on then the blankets again. The tie he wrapped around her ears, protecting the delicate lobes. He then proceeded to remove his pants. It amused him to note his bride turned her face to the side and wouldn't look. A pity she was so cold. He would have loved to see the heat of her blush.

With his aid, they pulled his pants on over hers then his socks, but she kept the running shoes she wore.

"When I'm done changing, I want you to get on my back and hold on tight." He kissed her cold lips when she seemed as if she might argue.

Naked, Dmitri didn't keep his human skin for long. He shifted, his furry self bounding forth, spreading the change. Fur sprouted, bones cracked and reshaped.

Some claimed it hurt. Pussies. Dmitri reveled in the strength of his inner beast.

His Siberian tiger with its plush coat, fluffy white mane around his head, and impressive striping burst free with a roar.

Cold, this isn't cold. His cat scoffed at the temperature, and with good reason as he was made for Russian winters.

He was also a big fucking feline, big enough to play pony to his chilly wife. She didn't require too much urging to get on. She draped herself on his back, her arms around his neck, her thighs hugging his sides. With her clamped on, he took off.

And she fell off.

Oops.

She managed a giggle as she sat up in the snow. "Guess riding a tiger isn't like riding a horse." She managed to say it without as much stuttering, her extra layers helping a little.

He chuffed.

Back on she climbed, this time holding tighter while he set off at a slower pace. It worked. She managed to stay on board. She nuzzled her face into the fur haloing his head.

While muffled, he still managed to understand her. "You have a mini mane. I thought only lions had those."

Lion manes weren't as soft and fluffy as his.

"Isn't there a limerick about a girl riding a tiger into the jungle, and the tiger coming back without her wearing a smile?"

Yeah. There was. But he'd explain that dirty limerick to her later. *Actually, maybe I'll show her.*

The forest didn't provide instant warmth once he reached it. However, it did help to diminish some of the cold wind trying to snatch their body heat.

The snow conspired to suck at his paws,

making each step annoyingly hard. If he were alone, he could have leapt and bounded to avoid the thicker spots, but with Teena on his back, he could only plod along.

He needed to find them a spot, a sheltered one where he could build them a fire, defend, and hopefully draw someone who would lead him to civilization.

We could also use a juicy rabbit.

His tiger, ever practical and thinking of his rumbling tummy.

The woods thinned as a rocky mound thrust up from the ground. Its rough stone surface mocked the snow's attempt to cling, but even better, about three-quarters of the way up, Dmitri spotted a ledge and a dark crevice. A cave if he was lucky.

But he couldn't climb it with her on his back. As if she sensed his dilemma, she slid off and stood.

"Are we both climbing, or did you want to check it out first?"

Dmitri was truly beginning to think he loved this woman. And he'd not even bedded her!

She possessed a level head and wits that appealed to him. She didn't require a thousand explanations—his damned sister whose favorite word was why—she didn't weep and wail—like his mother who lamented the fact that she'd never gone on the stage—and she didn't threaten to kill him—like his grandmother who never met a problem that violence wouldn't solve.

With a quick sniff to ensure nothing dangerous lurked, Dmitri then proceeded to climb the rocky hill.

The footing—or was that pawing, he could never be sure when it came to the English language—proved precarious. In a few spots, he felt himself slip, but he caught himself.

No looking foolish in front of his new wife.

Reaching the ledge he'd seen from the ground, he cocked his ears and listened. Nothing. He took a sniff and noted nothing fresh. The darkness he'd noted was indeed an opening. On quiet paws, he crept, in total stealth mode in case the cave already had an owner.

Bears might usually slumber this time of the year, but that didn't mean they wouldn't wake with the right incentive.

The cave proved bigger than he could have hoped for, stretching in for several yards and high enough that he might even be able to stand. While he did note some debris at the back, a mishmash of leaves, twigs, and small animals' bones, there was nothing recent, which meant they should be able to safely rest and warm up.

He turned around, and if he'd not been in tiger form, he might have yelped.

As it was, his tiger let out a pussyish "Meowr!" of surprise.

"Peekaboo, I followed you," claimed his wife, who'd successfully stalked him.

Chapter Sixteen

If a tiger could look surprised, then Dmitri's did. She couldn't help but laugh. "I guess the fact I was wearing your clothes made you not smell me coming. Too funny."

His blue eyes didn't appear amused.

And a few seconds later, neither was she.

A very naked Dmitri confronted her. How delightfully awesome. Slabs of muscle layered his arms and impressively wide chest. His torso narrowed at his hips, and he had a very interesting V that led down to—

Oh my. She averted her gaze and suddenly realized he was talking to her.

"Did you hear a word of what I just said?"

Should she lie? "No." Then perhaps it was the cold, or the fact that she'd almost died, a few times, but she blurted out the reason why. "I was distracted by your body."

His chest puffed out, and she noted the fur on it. Almost, she touched it.

"While your distraction is understandable, and appreciated, for future reference, I must point out that sneaking up on a predator of my caliber is foolhardy and dangerous. Don't do that again. I could have accidentally hurt you."

She snorted. "While I might not be as tough as my sister, I assure you I am not a delicate flower."

"Yes, you are."

"No, I'm not."

"Yes. You. Are." He glared at her.

She clamped her lips tight. Exactly why did she argue? She beamed. "Yes. I. Am."

Funny how agreeing with him brought such a look of astonishment to his face. "Little kitten, you are constantly surprising me."

"That's good, I hope."

"The best." He took a step closer, and how he could stand there naked, in a freezing cold cave, and still emit heat baffled her. She drifted toward him, the warmth of his body a gravitational pull, the smoky interest in his eyes a blood-warming promise, the buzz in her pocket an unwelcome distraction.

"Why are the pants you gave me vibrating?" she asked, looking down at her thigh.

"Damn. I forgot I stuffed my phone in there."

He groped her, not with erotic intent, alas, but on a quest for a cellphone that he pulled from the pocket with a triumphant aha, just as it stopped its buzz.

"The signal is weak, and my battery is low," he noted, holding it aloft and peering at it. "I am surprised we have any signal in this cave."

Teena would wager there usually wasn't any signal, but since Murphy was determined to have her expire a virgin, it didn't surprise her that he'd bent the rules and let the call interrupt.

What did shock her was that Dmitri headed back to the mouth of the cave and stood out on the ledge, naked in the buffeting wind.

"What are you doing?"

"Calling home, of course. I've only got one bar, but hopefully it is enough to—Sasha! My favorite sister. Yes, yes, I know you are my only sister, but that doesn't mean you're not my favorite." He paced the small ledge as he spoke, his hands moving with as much animation as his face.

"Why am I talking in English? Because, for one, we are both fluent in it, and secondly, I am not alone, and it would be rude to converse in Russian." He bobbed his head side to side. "No, I am not in enemy hands, being tortured, nor am I drunk." His brows shot up. "I resent that. I only ever rolled in that field of catnip once. I learned my lesson."

While Teena could only hear one side of the conversation, Dmitri's replies made it easy to imagine. "Yes, I know my plane dropped off the radar. I was in it when it crashed." He winced. "I'm obviously alive and surprisingly unhurt. I think my new wife is good luck."

Wow, did he ever have a skewed idea when it came to chance.

A squeal made him pull the phone from his ear. When it died down, he put it back to continue his conversation.

"Oh, did I forget to tell you about my wedding? It was a lovely, intimate affair. No, there were no guns involved." He grinned and winked at Teena. "Just drugs. But you'll be glad to know that she's fully conscious now and has yet to demand a divorce or make herself a widow. I think she likes me."

Teena couldn't help but giggle. It was true. She did like him. He was nuts. Impulsive. Totally sexy. *All mine.*

"So, before you start haranguing me again like a fish wife in the market—I do so know what a fish wife is. Just because I don't shop in the market doesn't mean I'm not knowledgeable." He went silent and rolled his eyes as a stream of words that she couldn't make out burst from the phone.

"Sasha, you need to listen for a moment. I don't know how long my phone will survive. I need you to come find me." He paused to listen. "What do you mean where? I am right here." He snickered at the rush of words that came from the phone. When it slowed down, he spoke again. "If I knew where here was, I wouldn't be lost. Yes, I know I'm a smartass. What can I say? I was blessed with both the looks and intelligence in our family."

Screech! His sister didn't take that one quietly.

Dmitri grinned, quite pleased with himself. "Sasha, enough of this chattering. I have to go. I think I see a bear. Or is that a lion? Rawr. No, I'm not kidding. My wife is a lion. And if you triangulate my cell signal and come fetch us, you can meet her before Mother gets her claws into her. Bye, little sister."

He hung up on her mid sentence and then tucked the phone on a rocky shelf at the cave entrance, probably to ensure the best possible signal for their rescuers.

She decided she shouldn't point out the flaws with him leaving it there. Given her history, they could expect a bird snatching it, a strong gust of wind carrying it, or a sudden earthquake sending it tumbling to smash on the rocks.

No need to destroy his optimism yet. If they did actually get rescued, he'd have plenty of time to regret getting hitched to her and to discover just how widespread her ill luck could get.

It took a special kind of man to ignore the way things constantly went wrong around her.

"Now that help is on the way"—he turned to her and clapped his hands together—"how about we get a fire going and begin the task of warming my bride?"

She could think of many ways to warm her. Not all them required actual fire.

"Let me fetch some wood."

Once again, she took a page from her much dirtier-minded sister and let her gaze drop. She could almost hear Meena say, "Now that's what I call some serious wood." Indeed, her husband's manparts seemed very happy to have her looking. To her wide-eyed gaze, his erection thickened, largely so.

Too large surely for... She peeked down at herself and blushed at his knowing chuckle.

"Fear not, little kitten. When the time comes, it will fit. Snugly. Perfectly."

She swallowed.

He noticed, and was it possible for his smile to become even more devilish? "Stay here out of the wind while I fetch some kindling."

"But you're naked."

"Then I best be quick."

He was, darting down the rocky hillside with more agility than any human man possessed. He snapped off branches instead of foraging, their crack loud in the silent woods.

When he returned, after nearly making her heart stop as he precariously leaped and balanced on his poor bare feet, his arms laden with sticks, she said, "So how many parts are you going to lose to frostbite?"

He winked as he said, "I only have one blue body part, and it isn't the cold threatening it."

What a gift he owned for turning everything sexual. Or was it her reading innuendo into everything?

As he stacked branches at the cave entrance, she had to wonder if a fire was their smartest course. "Shouldn't we worry about the guys who shot down our plane finding us via the smoke?"

"Worry? Never."

"You think they'll assume we died in the crash?"

"I hope not."

"Excuse me?"

Dmitri paused in his placement of the sticks. He shot her a look, the hank of hair dropping over his brow managing to exude a wild elegance that ignored the fact he was kneeling naked in the freezing cold. "I am expecting them to come after us. I want them to. How else will I discover who has the nerve to attack me? How else will I retaliate?"

"But what if they outnumber us or have weapons?"

"A man likes a challenge. Now dig around in my pocket there, would you? I should have a keychain in there.

She located the cold metal and yanked it free. Dmitri took it from her as he strode past to the back of the cave. He returned with his arms cradled to hold a pile of crumbling leaves and brittle bones. He dumped them on his woodpile before he knelt again.

Dangling from his keychain was a cylinder. Wait, not a cylinder but a lighter.

Dmitri twisted the safety cap on the butane lighter and ignited it.

"You carry around a lighter? What for?" Most shifters had a healthy respect for fire. While most lived in civilized homes, some of their history had seen them fleeing before the voracious appetite of a flame. Because of this innate fear and respect of fire, most kept away from it.

Not Dmitri. He waved the flame over dried sticks, their surface damp with melting snow. "Aha, time for me to divulge a dirty secret. I used to smoke cigarettes when I was younger. It drove my mother nuts."

She wrinkled her nose. "Ew. Cigarettes smell."

"Only to those who don't smoke them."

"Do you still smoke?"

"Not anymore."

"You came to your senses about your health."

He snorted. "No. I miss them every day. But I lost a damned bet to my mother, and she won't allow a rematch."

"What game did you play?"

"Tiger Is Coming, of course. I lay under that table we were playing at for almost two days trying to recover."

"I can't believe your mother outdrank you."

"And soundly too. The woman was nursed on vodka." Said with fond pride.

"Drinking has nothing to do with smoking, though, so I still don't get why you keep a lighter around."

"Because I also like to set things on fire." He winked. "That's something you'll discover as soon as we manage to make it to a bed."

"Why do we need a bed?"

"Because I will not take your virginity like some impatient youth on the floor of a dirty cave."

Given the smells in the place, she could kind of see his point, but still, couldn't he improvise? "What's wrong with the wall?"

She'd wager it probably wasn't often Dmitri was left speechless. Look at how cute he was with his jaw hanging open in disbelief.

"The wall is not a proper place to breach you the first time," he finally sputtered.

"You know, in all the times my sister cursed and swore about you, she never mentioned the fact that you were a prude."

"I am not a prude. Merely determined to make your first experience a memorable one."

"And you don't think having sex in a cave after having our plane shot down is memorable enough?" She arched a brow.

"No," he growled.

He held his hands out to the flickering flame that struggled to burn the cold, and damp, wood.

Smoke curled from the pile, but given he'd made the fire at the entrance to the cave, it was sucked outside instead of in. What did radiate in was a feeble warmth.

Dumping the blankets from her shoulders, she placed them on the dirt-encrusted ground, sat, removed the sharp rock right under her left buttock, and then sat again.

Dmitri didn't quite sit beside her. He sprawled on his back, head in her lap, and grinned. "Hello, little kitten."

She frowned. "Hello?"

"Do you realize this is our honeymoon night?"

"No, it's not. I slept through it on the flight over, remember? Needle. Ass. Snoring away."

"That didn't count. The honeymoon night is the first *conscious* night we spend together as a married couple."

"And you just randomly decided this?"

"Not randomly. Quite deliberately." How adorable his smug smile.

"So given this is our honeymoon night, does this mean you've given up on your whole needs-a-bed plan?"

"Only for certain parts. You know, there are other things we can do in preparation for the main event."

"Really? Like what?" Virgin didn't mean Teena couldn't come up with some pretty good scenarios. Kissing, petting, skin-to-skin nakedness...

"We should get to know each other."

"Excuse me?"

"Tell me about yourself. What is your favorite color?"

"Red."

"Really? Mine is yellow, which I know seems quite odd, and yet I find it quite soothing."

Who cared about her favorite color when all she wanted to know was what his lips tasted like.

I thought we already knew that answer.

Fine, she wanted a refresher.

"Are we really doing this?" she asked.

"Yes. And it's your turn. Do you have a question?"

"How about how long do you figure before we make it to a bed?"

His nostrils flared. "Kitten, while I appreciate your impatience, please note this is just as hard for me as you. I might even say *harder.*"

She found her eyes drawn to the part of him that he referred to. Despite his reassurance, it was pretty damned big. Perhaps he had a point about holding off. What if he was wrong and she required medical attention after?

For distraction she said, "Boxers or briefs?"

"Such a dirty mind with only one direction. Absolutely delightful. But the answer is none. Now my turn, do you like chips or chocolate? Me, I'm a fellow with a sweet tooth."

"Chips. And this is stupid."

"No, it's not. Look at how much we are discovering. Do you—"

Since she couldn't convince her idiot husband to seduce her, time to take matters in her own hands. Or, in this case, lips.

Crouching over to press her mouth to his might not have been the most comfortable pose, but the electric touch of their lips made up for it.

"You know," he said in between nibbles, "perhaps we could cuddle."

Cuddling sounded—"Eep." She yelled in surprise as he rolled from her lap, seated himself, and dragged her onto him all before she could mutter a husky, "Dmitri."

"Say it again."

Facing him, she couldn't hold his gaze, not when it smoldered so hotly. "Dmitri." She whispered it, but he still groaned.

"Why is it, when you talk, I want to crush you in my arms and devour you?"

"I wish you would."

"Which surprises me, little kitten. You are untouched. I am virtually a stranger. An enemy really in your family's eyes. And yet, you would give yourself to me."

"To my husband."

"A husband who forced you to marry him. Most women, especially Russian ones like my sister, would have gutted me with a knife by now and made herself a widow. Yet you…" He stroked her cheek. "You, my precious kitten, you beg me to take you. You stress the limits of my patience. You fill me with a burning desire. I do not understand it."

"People would say it's fate."

"Fate is us discovering one another in the first place. This connection I sense between us… It is—"

"Frightening?"

"Never. More like awe-inspiring. Precious. *Mine.*" He growled the word against her lips before taking them in a torrid kiss. His hand spanned the back of her neck, holding her close while his fingers threaded her messy strands.

The fire at her back warmed but not as much as he did, the heat from his body scorching through her layers, teasing her with the fiery passion that simmered between them.

His lips left hers and blazed a trail across her cheek, to her ear, down her neck. "Oh, Dmitri." She breathed his name as her head tilted back and her eyes shut.

Liquid fire coursed through her veins as he touched her. More than anything so simple as touch, he awakened all her senses. Ignited her desire.

I want.

She wanted more than just kisses.

Her turn to clutch his face and bring her mouth against his for a hungry embrace. Their tongues dueled. Their breathing meshed. Their hearts raced as blood pounded through their veins.

She grumbled at their position and pushed at his shoulders. He lay on his back for her, dragging her with him so she lay atop. Much better. She could now feel the length of him. Hard muscles were hers to explore, and she did, her hands skimming the skin that had lost all its earlier chill.

She didn't need sexual experience to know he enjoyed her touch. Nor did she need any help when it came to pleasing him. She simply pleased herself, allowing herself to explore and ignoring his protests.

"Kitten, we shouldn't."

"I don't care if we don't have a bed," she grumbled.

"I do, but that's not the real issue. Aah. Aah." He lost his train of thought for a moment, probably because she'd found the ridge of his nipple.

She bit it. He liked it.

So she did it again.

"I should have nicknamed you little devil. Tempting me like this."

"Is that bad?"

He rolled them, his movements careful and gentle, but the end result was he ended up on top.

She wiggled under his weight. He groaned. "How did I get so lucky?"

"Shh." She dragged him down for a kiss. "Don't jinx it."

Words were lost and forgotten as they embraced, but with him atop her, the experience took on a new level for her.

His body nestled between her parted thighs, and despite her dual layers, she felt him. Hard. Thick. And pressing against her sex.

Her breath hitched. He rubbed again, and she made a sound, a sound he caught with his lips. His hand quested under the fabric of her shirt, reaching up to grasp and tweak her nipple.

A gasp escaped her then a moan of pleasure as he rolled the erect nub, teasing it into a hard point.

She'd never imagined how it would feel to have someone else caress her. She'd naïvely thought her own exploratory caresses of her body were it. That foreplay was just a pleasant thing.

How wrong she was. How delightfully wrong.

When his skin brushed hers, she felt it like a

brand upon her body. When his fingers tweaked her bud, it sent a jolt of aching desire right to her sex.

As for when he pushed her shirt high enough to latch his mouth around the tip...

"Dmitri!" She might have screamed his name, the sensation proved so electric.

A rumble vibrated her flesh in his mouth as he chuckled. "So sweet."

So enjoying his touch he should have said.

She arched her back, her body knowing what to do and that was get more of what felt good.

His mouth tugged and sucked at her breast. His tongue swirled decadently.

She cried out when he let go with a wet, popping sound, only to moan as he poured his attention into arousing her other breast.

But that wasn't the only thing he wanted to lick. His mouth tickled and burned its way down her stomach, tracing her curves in a path that took him to the waistband of her pants. They didn't deter him.

His fingers tugged the fabric and slid under the elastic.

She sucked in a breath.

The tickle of his fingers through the fur on her mound had her panting. Her hips quivered, and she ached. Ached for something.

Him.

She screamed his name for a second time as he found her slick sex, his rougher fingers stroking along the sensitive curve of her nether lips. A moan escaped, and she clamped her lip with her teeth as he delicately spread her. He seesawed a finger back and forth across her moist cleft.

Her thighs clamped tight over his hand, holding him against her, and her hips arched, pressing against it.

"Easy, kitten. You make it hard for me to be gentle."

'Maybe I don't want gentle," she growled.

"Then I'm succeeding in my wooing," he murmured against her belly before placing a kiss.

He withdrew his hand from her pants, and she almost cried—*Why are you punishing me?*—until she realized he needed his hand to work her track pants over her hips and down to her thighs.

The air in the cave had warmed, whether from the fire or his actions she couldn't have said, but despite her exposed skin, she didn't shiver from cold. She did, however, shudder with expectation.

Who wouldn't when bright blue eyes stared at her denuded bottom end with such hunger?

And it seemed he meant to quench his need for her. She sucked in a breath and yet couldn't find it to exclaim much more than a squeaked "Dmitri!"

As if her feeble protest would stop this man on a mission. Between her legs, he nestled his face, and all so he could lap at her with a warm tongue.

Warm, slightly raspy, and oh dear god. That felt so fucking good.

Back and forth he licked her, the wet tip of his tongue stimulating as it found her hooded clit for play. When her cries became too strident, and her hips too arched, he let his tongue travel to the entrance of her sex, where he probed at her until she sobbed his name.

Then back to her swollen button he went, teasing her. Pleasuring her. Driving her to the bridge and...

Aaaah. She fell over an edge, an ecstatic plunge into orgasm that shook her body and wrung her with waves of utmost pleasure.

It took her a moment to come back down from

such climactic heights, but when she did, she found herself cradled in his arms, his lips pressing soft kisses against her temple as he murmured to her softly in Russian.

"That was..." Words failed her, so she sighed.

He chuckled. "I know."

"That's arrogant."

"It's not arrogant to state the truth. You enjoyed that."

She wouldn't lie. "Yes, I did. And see, we didn't need a bed." She wiggled against him, her sensitive parts very much attuned to the fact that he still pressed hard and erect against her.

"I will not have it said that I debauched you in a dirty cave."

Stubborn man, but given the glow suffusing her, she'd allow it. But that didn't mean he shouldn't get a prize in return. Maybe incentive to give up his foolish idea.

She pushed at his shoulders, and he complied, rolling onto his back and bringing her with him so she lay splayed across him.

However, much as she liked the feel of him against her, she had a different goal in mind.

Getting to her knees, she braced her palms on either side of his chest and leaned in to place soft kisses on his skin.

Kisses with a destination.

"Kitten, what are you doing?"

Wasn't it obvious? She'd read enough books to have a pretty good idea of what to do once she reached his throbbing shaft. She couldn't wait to experiment...and taste.

Nothing like the click of a weapon being primed to stop a girl from going south.

And to piss a tiger off.

Chapter Seventeen

He dies. Slowly. Painfully. Maybe a day for each second of annoyance and torture I am suffering.

As soon as Teena began her innocent exploration, Dmitri pretty much decided to hell with waiting for a bed. Teena was ready for him to claim her, and he was more than ready for her.

The honeyed taste of her sex still sweetened his lips. The vibration of her orgasm still tickled his tongue. She was determined to return the favor.

And this asshat just had to go and interrupt. Totally unacceptable.

Heedless of his nakedness—and still raging erection that bobbed majestically—he rose from the hard ground. With a glare, he fixed the intruder, who continued to point a gun at them and leer.

Does he dare to look at my woman? Does he truly dare to lust after my wife?

It wasn't only his tiger that thought he should tear the eyes from this man's sockets. The man found himself in the grips of jealousy the likes of which he'd never experienced, not even when his mother bought his sister that wondrous Mercedes SI500 on her twenty-first birthday.

A step sideways provided a shield for his wife in the form of his body. Behind him, he could hear Teena righting her clothing. He could practically feel the heat of her embarrassment.

Worry not, little kitten. I shall protect your honor.

"I think I caught some pussy cats."

The human got one thing right. They were cats. But caught?

I beg to differ.

Sneaking up on Dmitri while he was majorly distracted was one thing. Actually prevailing?

Not today.

"Do you know that my family, centuries ago, used to celebrate their conquests by eating the flesh of their enemies?" Dmitri took a step forward.

"Fucking animals."

As if he'd not heard the insult, Dmitri smiled. "It is said that devouring the flesh of our foes steals their honor and strength for our own."

"Bloodthirsty bastards."

"Yes, yes we were. Are. Do you know what my grandmother remembers best of those years before the higher councils banned it? Just how good human blood tastes." Dmitri lunged with a snarl more beast than man.

Funny how a firearm wasn't always the best defense. The idiot in the entrance to the cave could have fired it. Swung it as a bat. Even sidestepped the forward thrust of Dmitri's body.

However, fear was a funny thing, especially in humans. Fear made people not always react most efficiently. Fear had only one instinct—survival.

The guy, with the gun in hand, spun on his heel and uttered a very unmanly squeak. Dmitri's lips stretched into a feral grin.

"Dinner!" he practically sang as he dove after the human.

So here was the thing about climbing rocks, covered in snow and ice, in the dark while a strong breeze whistled and tugged. For those who weren't surefooted, say like a certain human terrified out of his mind, it could prove treacherous.

Slip. "Aaaah." *Thud.* "Oomph." *Crash.* Silence.

Head cocked, Dmitri leaned over the ledge and regarded the body at the bottom of the incline. "Dammit. I'd hoped to question him."

Peering over his shoulder, Teena pressed against his back. Once again, his wife proved her worth. "You should grab his clothes before they get wet."

A practical woman. He could have pressed her against the wall of the cave and taken her, right then and there.

But…the moment was lost. Their enemy had found them, and although they'd defeated one, more possibly followed.

Together they made their way down the mountain, him offering his lady a helping hand, which she took with a smile.

As for when she lost her footing, landed on him, and they both fell back in a cold drift of snow? The snow in unmentionable places proved unpleasant, but the warm laughter against his lips and the soft kiss more than made up for it.

Pleasant as it was, though, they couldn't waste time melting the snowbank. He'd gotten caught off guard once. He couldn't allow it again.

It took a few attempts, and some laughter, before they managed to make it to their feet and out of the deep drift. He didn't argue about taking some of the clothes. Even for someone who'd practiced cold-weather survival—just one of the training camps his mother had sent him on to prepare him for life as a leader—he knew he needed some clothes.

In the end, they shared the gear, the boots too

small for his feet, the jacket barely large enough to span his width, but the shirt fit well over the bulk she wore, and the hat kept her head snug.

"Ready?" he asked.

"For what?" was her reply. Bright-cheeked and clear-eyed, she regarded him. Her lips seemed to hold a permanent little smile. A result of their earlier pleasure?

As if there was any question.

He shouldered the strap of the rifle and then grasped her gloved hands. "We have to leave."

"What happened to staying and waiting for your sister while holding off the enemy?"

"Shifters have a certain honor. At least in Russia. If a group had come after me, our battles would have taken place, one on one. Easy."

"What if there's like four or five? Fighting that many, even one after another, isn't what I'd call easy."

He arched a brow. "If you think that, then you should come to my training. Since a young age, my mother has had me fighting the best. The wiliest."

"And yet I hear Leo got the better of you in that fight at the club."

Her smile took the sting out of her insult. But he bristled. He didn't want her to think him weak. "You wound me, kitten. Did it never occur to anyone I let him win? By that point I knew I didn't want your sister, and yet, to say so would have meant me losing face. A man has a reputation to uphold."

"So you threw a fight?"

"I let the omega of the pride I was hosting with, a rather large, intimidating man, come out only slightly ahead in our altercation before your sister interrupted."

"Okay, cocky one, if you think you can take on that many shifters, then why does a group of humans scare you?"

"Because of these." He indicated the gun. "These take the honor out of the equation. These could seriously hurt you."

"And you."

"Bah. Scars make a man."

"Crazy," she said the word softly with a little laugh.

"Russian."

Was it him, or did he hear "mine" whispered softly?

For a moment, he was tempted to stay. He wanted to peel the layers from her and indulge in the beauty of her. But some things were more important than quick pleasure, such as her survival.

More warmly attired, they headed away from their temporary shelter. He led the way, eyes and ears scanning the deep shadows around them, only dimly illuminated by the sliver of moonlight in the sky.

The wind might prove brisk, but the air itself had warmed in the hours since their crash.

Good, and yet bad. They wouldn't have to fight the frigid chill that liked to cling to bones and take limbs prisoner. However, warmer temps meant possible melting. Fluffy flakes brushed off; clingy, damp snow soaked.

Reaching the bottom of the hill, he closed his eyes for a moment and tilted his face to the sky. He inhaled deeply, sifting the scents. Wintertime was the worst when it came to scents. The air, so crisp, did not hold scent well. The many layers humans, and even shifters, wore masked their innate musk. It made tracking so much harder.

On the upside, at least there were prints in the snow. His and Teena's, flashing beacons to whoever tracked them, and then there were those of the dead man.

He followed them, and Teena hissed. "What are you doing? Shouldn't we move away from the bad guys?"

"This bad guy didn't walk all the way here. He had some kind of vehicle. I want it."

"You think he drove?"

"Or..." Dmitri smiled as they came across the team of dogs and the sled, the only way to truly travel out here in silence. Snowmobiles, with their loud, growly motors, tended to warn people miles away, especially in the open places.

With a good team of dogs, other than a whisk of runners on snow, they were death on silent wings.

Beside him, Teena stiffened. "Are those dogs?"

"A team of pure-bred huskies. Well trained, too. See how they wait without a tether to anchor them for a signal."

"Um, I think I should warn you. Dogs act funny around me."

She stepped behind him, and he wondered at her trepidation. Had she suffered an incident with canines as a child? She was a cat. Perhaps it was some kind in innate leonine fear? Oddly enough, despite the fact she hid behind him, he didn't smell fear from her. More...apology?

Apology for what?

It began with one whine then two. Then it seemed the entire team of Siberian huskies took up the sound. Some sat. Others stood and wagged their tails while a few projected a mean set of puppy dog eyes.

"What the hell are they doing?"

"Loving me." Teena smiled as she approached them, and if they could have died with tail-thumping happiness, they would have. The moment she got close enough, these big, trained dogs, with massive teeth, were wiggling around and yipping in ecstasy as she did her best to stroke and scratch them all.

"There's my good puppies. Who's so handsome? What a soft belly you have. Do you need a tickle?"

Was it wrong for him to be so jealous of some dumb dogs?

He moved to approach, and as one, the team raised their heads, pivoted in his direction, and fixed him with eyes glaring with baleful intent. A few had their lips curled. And, yes, that was definitely the sound of growling.

"Are they seriously threatening me?" He blinked. He was a freaking tiger. Dogs did not menace him.

Leaning forward, he let his wild side rise to the surface and growled back.

That shut them up, but they also clustered closer to his wife and kept close watch on him.

"My little kitten, a dog whisperer. Your various levels are vastly intriguing. Just what other surprises do you hide?"

"You'll have to find out. So, is this our ticket out of here?"

He bowed and swept his hands toward the sled. "Your chariot awaits."

As they clambered aboard, Dmitri noted a strapped bag at the front end of the sled. Kneeling, he opened it and found more clothing, as well as a few protein bars and a warm flask.

As they sipped the hot coffee, laced with something that fired the belly, Teena stared at the travois behind the sled, the one with straps.

"Is it me," she said, "or does that look like it's made to carry a body?"

"You are correct, wife."

"So whoever sent this guy after us wanted him to bring something back."

"You mean someone. The question is, was he supposed to bring us back dead or alive?"

"Given the hijacking, I'd say alive, but—"

"Expendable if we can't be taken. Someone is playing a dangerous game."

"What will you do?"

Dmitri couldn't help but smile. "Change the rules of course. I don't like to lose."

Chapter Eighteen

If someone would have told Teena a few days ago she'd be dressed in a dead man's castoffs, hugging her husband's waist as they whipped through some Russian woods while being pulled by a team of dogs, she would have laughed and said never. That type of wild adventure was more Meena's style.

Except Meena had nothing to do with this adventure.

Teena was the one living and enjoying this crazy new reality.

While mishaps continued to befall her, Dmitri stuck by her side. He took the bad luck in stride and even faced it with a grin.

He always had a grin, an adorable tilt of his lips that she could just kiss, again and again. She inadvertently hugged him tighter.

"Patience, little kitten," he muttered over his shoulder, his words short-lived as the wind whipping their faces stole them away. "We will find true shelter soon."

"Or?"

"There is no or."

"You're so optimistic."

"Dwelling on the negative accomplishes nothing. Plotting victory, on the other hand, brings success."

"What about when you fail?"

"Then you plan again. Failure only happens

when you give up."

An interesting philosophy. One that the humans hunting them also followed.

They also wouldn't give up.

Their only warning was a crack and then a whizzing sound as a bullet flew past their faces and hit the bark of a tree with explosive results.

Splinters flew as the dry exterior shredded at the impact.

"Get down," Dmitri yelled.

Down would provide some element of cover, or at least less of a target, but what of Dmitri? He stood straight and tall on the sled, his hands holding the reins with assurance.

Another booming sound as someone fired again. This one scored a line across Dmitri's hand, yet crouched below him, she noted he did not cry out, merely sucked in a breath even though it had to hurt. He bled. She could smell it, and yet he did not allow his injured hand to relinquish its grip.

Hearing a shout, she turned to peer behind them. While the shadows made it hard to make out fine details, she noted the team of dogs barreling after them. A glint of pale moonlight off a barrel made her shout, "Behind us!"

With a snap of the reins and a sharp tug, their dogsled veered to the left, their rugged chariot tilting on one side before thumping down hard again as they raced in a new direction.

They hit a major bump, and she lost her grip. She went airborne for a moment. Then hit the bottom hard, and she felt herself sliding. She scrambled for a handhold, but they hit another lump, and this time when she soared, she ended up right out of the sled.

Splat.

Okay, so her landing in the snowy bank wasn't puddle-wet, but the white stuff was clinging, and her location also put her in the path of the other dogsled!

Eyes wide, she stared at the approaching animals. Then she closed them. She didn't have time to move and escape the certain trampling.

Huff. Puff. The panting animals neared. Neared. Passed.

The sound receded, and she opened her eyes to see she lived.

Pushing to her knees, sinking a little farther, she shook her head to dislodge the sticky flakes. The air held its breath. Silent.

And lonely.

This probably wasn't good.

Dmitri will come back for me.

If he could.

Wouldn't it figure that once again, disaster had struck. But, this time, it really chose a doozy.

"Thanks a lot, Murphy." She grumbled as she followed the tracks of the dogsleds. "I realize the universe wants to screw me of my happily ever after, but really?" She stopped a moment and glared at the sky. "If you were going to kill me, couldn't you have done it at the beach instead of in the middle of some freaking cold woods?"

As if he didn't like her reply, she noted the hum of an engine, a snowmobile engine, which meant it wasn't Dmitri. The noise echoed around her, and she couldn't tell from which direction it came.

She tried to run along the path, in the direction her husband had gone. Safety in numbers, or behind a broad back, as her daddy used to like to tell her with a wink when she was little.

However, the clear trail, while easier to travel,

also acted like a guided map to whoever rode the snowmobile.

A bright light shone behind her, the glare blinding after all the darkness. She turned and headed off the path, but the snow proved deeper and softer than expected. She sank to her hips.

She couldn't move. It made her inner feline practically whimper. Bad enough it was cold, but now trapped too?

The snowmobile approached, the growl of its motor loud and the light brighter than ever.

When it stopped, only yards from her, the glare proved so intense she had to throw an arm over her eyes.

But worse was knowing it wasn't Dmitri coming toward her saying, "What do we have here?"

Chapter Nineteen

Dmitri's first impulse when Teena flew off the sled was to stop and turn around, except there was no turning around, not here where the trees clustered making any kind of sharp veer dangerous.

Not to mention, their pursuers had bypassed his wife to come after him.

Let them come after me instead of her. He'd have to trust she could handle herself while he took care of business. Speaking of taking care of...

He timed his jump just right, leaping from the moving sled to the thick branch hanging overhead.

Swinging onto it, he crouched, a predator in the dark waiting for his prey.

And there came his intended victims, their team of dogs leading the way, the sled slightly larger than his and carrying two men.

How sporting.

In silence, Dmitri dropped onto them.

Two humans against one cat. Not great odds, for them.

Their shrill yelps of surprise were annoyingly short. He killed them too quickly.

Now how will they tell the rest of their friends I'm here and hunting?

He tossed their bodies from the slowing sled. The dogs without a hand guiding them on the rein trotted and then walked themselves to a halt.

Stripping the men quickly of their warm gear

and weapons, he whistled at the dogs as he tugged at the lead. They turned at his command, obedient to the universal signals they taught instead of to a single person.

Before he could get them into motion and heading back toward Teena, a voice from behind stopped him.

"Hello there, kitty. Leaving so soon?"

Leave when someone begged for an ass-kicking? Never.

Dmitri dropped the reins and whirled to see someone clad in white and gray camouflage step from behind a tree, rifle aimed right at him.

"Here, human, human. Come to papa kitty," Dmitri crooned.

In most opponents, this provoked a rage at his blatant disrespect. Not this fellow. He also didn't play with honor or by the rules. He shot from a distance. Dmitri ignored the tiny sting. It would take more than that to fell him.

"Coward. Come closer so that I can smite you."

But the human remained out of reach. And laughed. Laughed most mockingly damn him.

The blow to his honor almost staggered Dmitri. His mother would surely weep in disgrace. But only if he failed to kill the human insulting him.

Of course, murderous plans worked better if a tiger stayed awake. Several darts hit him at once, and while they weren't bullets, they were tipped in a sleeping agent, enough to take his big ass down.

I think I understand now why little kitten was a tad annoyed, the loss of control sucked, and nothing could stop the sucking darkness.

Chapter Twenty

The "What do we have here?" was spoken by a woman, even if that wasn't immediately discernible with the heavy goggles, Russian hat on her head, and thick fur coat with its fluffy collar.

"Are you going to kill me?" Teena figured she might as well get the question out of the way.

"Depends. Are you part of the plot to kill my brother?"

"Who's your brother?"

Moving the goggles to sit atop her head, the blue-eyed woman bore a strong resemblance to a certain missing husband.

"You're Dmitri's sister."

"Yes, I am Sasha. And you must be his new wife," she said, eyeballing Teena with a frown. "Is it me, or do you look remarkably like my brother's last fiancée?"

"Probably because I'm Meena's twin sister."

"Twin?" Sash snickered. "Trust my brother to not give up. And it's true, you're married?"

"Yes."

"He mentioned he'd acquired a new bride, yet neglected to tell us who. I see why now."

"It was kind of sudden," was Teena's reply.

"So I heard," Sasha said with a snicker. "I am surprised to find you alone. Where is my brother? There is no way he'd allow you to wander off on your own."

The remark might have stung if Teena didn't sense the anxiety in the words. "I fell off the dog sled."

"And Dmitri did not return for you?" Dark brows arched high.

"He was kind of busy trying to stay out of reach of the guys chasing him and shooting."

Sasha took a moment to absorb this information before replying, "I see the curse that follows your sister also tags along with you."

"Yeah."

"Excellent. Dmitri could use a little excitement in his life. Now enough talk. I must go and rescue my brother. Stay here and wait. Another of my team will swing around to pick you up." Sasha tossed her a black box she pulled from a pocket. "Hold on to this. It's a tracking device. It will help them find you."

"Why can't I go with you?"

"With me? Why would we do that?"

"To rescue Dmitri of course."

"You want him saved?" Blue eyes fixed her with an intense stare she knew all too well.

"Yes. Of course I do. He's my husband."

For some reason her reply seemed to please Sasha because she beamed at her. "Come, my new sister. Let us follow the tracks and see where they lead us."

Where they led was to a trampled scene but no Dmitri.

Sasha grumbled as she surveyed the tracks. "Taken by humans. Mother will have a litter of kittens."

Indeed, Dmitri's mother proved less than impressed at the news. "The shame. The horror. My son, brought low by"—her lips curled—"humans. His father is surely turning in his grave."

"You had him cremated, mother," was Sasha's reply.

They were currently in a large tent, made to withstand the cold. When a brisk wind and thick falling snow covered the tracks, they had to call it quits. They regrouped at the base camp Dmitri's mother set up, a mother who was less than impressed when she met Teena.

"You! What nerve you have to come back after leaving my poor boy bereft at the altar."

Teena sighed. "That wasn't me. That was my twin sister."

"No matter. Same family which means you will probably desert him too."

"Actually, I want to help save him."

"You want to help?" His mother snorted. "I find that hard to believe. More likely you would allow my poor little Dmitri to die that you might become a widow and escape him like your misguided sister."

"I would never do that." Teena didn't need to feign indignation.

"Why not? You did not come into this marriage willingly. I will wager your family is actively searching for you, and that means you must have done something to trigger their unease. Perhaps you've secretly called them for rescue? Are they the ones behind the abduction and ransom of my son?"

"My family wouldn't have done all those things. My dad might be a tad violent at times"— understatement of the year—"but he would never put me in harm's way, just like he wouldn't hurt my husband." She hoped.

"Is he your husband?"

"More or less. I mean, we had a priest do his thing, and we signed the papers. We just haven't gotten to the consummation part, which I assure you is not for lack of trying. Since I'm a virgin, Dmitri keeps insisting we do it right. Something about ensuring the experience lives up to expectation." The brandy Sasha had fed her from a flask had done more than warm her chilled bones; it loosened her tongue.

"I don't believe it," Sasha interjected with a snort. "Big brother has stage fright. That's priceless."

"But not important at the moment. We must plan his release."

Teena took another swig of the courage in a bottle. "How can we plan his release if we don't know where he is? Did you receive a ransom or a clue as to his whereabouts?"

"There will be no ransom." The mother waved a hand in dismissal.

"What do you mean no ransom? Don't you have enough to pay it?"

"First, none was requested. And second..." Sasha looked at her mother, and they both burst out laughing. "Pay? We would never pay a single ruble to our enemies."

"You'd let him die instead?" Teena wondered if she looked as appalled as she sounded.

"Bah. Dmitri isn't going to die. We have a plan."

Talking to these women was like pulling teeth. Slow and agonizing. "And the plan is?"

"We rescue him of course."

So matter-of-fact about it all, and yet Teena foresaw one big problem. "How can you rescue him when you don't know where he is?"

"We don't know yet, but we will. We are waiting for the satellite to get in the right position again. GPS tracking in an organic host is still in the test phase. In order to render the chips small enough to avoid detection, they are harder to track and need a very directed satellite coordinate."

"You had him microchipped? Like a household pet?" Teena gaped at Dmitri's mother.

"Do not get her started," Sasha muttered. "She thinks it's appalling that not everyone chips their kid but will ensure the protection of Fido and Fluffy."

"So how long before this satellite comes into position?" How long until they could go and rescue Dmitri? Funny how she harbored no thoughts about his demise or how easy it would be to let matters run their course. She wanted him back. Wanted to give this whole marriage thing a whirl.

Somehow in their short courtship, she'd come to forget he'd dated Meena first. Actually, the more she heard about Dmitri and her sister, the more she noted how unsuited they were.

No one seemed to approve of that pairing, and yet was it her, or did she and Dmitri share an entirely different rapport? Teena could easily admit she liked him, and she was going to go out on a limb and say he liked her, too. She didn't care what her family would think or say.

He'd told her enough times and shown her in enough ways that she meant something to him. Even more astonishing, she got the sneaky suspicion that his sister and mother liked her, too, at least once they'd discerned she truly didn't want him to die.

No dying allowed, which was why when Sasha said, "We should be able to grab his signal, if he's not halfway across the planet, in the next eight hours," Teena knew she had to act.

"Eight hours?" Teena couldn't help but repeat. "No, we can't wait that long. Who knows what they could do to him in that period of time?"

"Then what do you suggest? We already have teams driving in circles around his last known position. The storm is making it impossible to find him."

Outside she heard a shout, followed by a sharp bark.

Teena stumbled from the tent, forgetting to zip her jacket or grab a hat. She didn't want to delay, not if she'd heard right.

Stepping into the whirling mini storm, the flakes sticking damply to her skin, she blinked and then smiled.

"Hello there. Did you come find me?" Taking a few steps forward, she held her hand out to the leader of the dog sled. His one blue eye and one yellow one regarded her steadily.

She stroked her hand over his muzzle. "Such a good boy. Very smart, too. Smart enough to find me in a storm. And I'll bet smart enough to find his way home."

The low snarl from the pack leader wasn't needed for Teena to know Sasha had joined her.

"What are these?" she asked.

Teena smiled. "These are our ticket to finding my husband."

Chapter Twenty-one

With much yawning and stretching, Dmitri roused from his drug-induced slumber. At least his tiger did, and it seemed determined to make the man wake too.

Ever experienced the mental version of a bitch slap by big, hairy paws? It proved abrupt, but it also worked.

He seemed to be moving, just not using his own two feet. A pair of large men carried him, actually more like dragged, one to each arm. His eyes refused to stay open, the effects of the drugs lingering. In between blinks he caught sight of stone, more stone, oh and he thought he smelled a rat. The human kind, not the squeaky.

Abruptly, the moving stopped. The fellows gripping him tossed him forward. The hard floor almost smashed his nose, but instinct had him throwing out his hands and hitting the surface with his palms instead of his face.

Rude. Did those who manhandled him not know who he was?

I should tell them. As soon as he managed to shrug this lethargic slumber. No wonder Teena seemed a touch annoyed at his repeated use of narcotics. The sensation of not being in control well and truly sucked.

No more drugging my wife. Unless it was with kisses.

Dragging open heavy eyelids, Dmitri heard the

clang of a metal-rimmed door getting slammed shut. In that moment, the loud sound proved a tie for nails on chalkboard. He still shuddered at the thought of his sister, a smirk on her face, dragging her fingers down the matte surface, doing her best to irritate him. It worked. So he retaliated. Her shrieks of outrage totally made up for the weeks he'd spent polishing silverware until he could see himself in it.

Head pounding, eyes gritty, and mouth in need of a stiff, alcoholic drink—all lovely side effects—did not prevent him from standing. And leaning. Damned floor tilted.

A crack of one lid allowed him a peek to take stock of his location. Dreary, and yet classic. *Look at that, they stuck the savage shapeshifter in a dungeon. Idiots.*

Did they not do their homework?

Know thy enemy. A lesson taught on every knee of every adult he'd ever been bounced on.

To know every minute detail of a foe was to prevent getting screwed by them. Take now, for example. Had his captor done his due diligence, he would have known Dmitri's favorite play area as a child was the dungeon—although it took a few times where his mother tossed him in a cell and said, "Come find me for a treat," before he appreciated the entertainment value.

Such fun family times.

He took stock of his surroundings. While this dungeon didn't belong to him, the archaic design, with its flaws and strengths, was familiar.

Hello, cell, my old friend. His current room had no window. A shame, those types of cells were the easiest to escape from. Pop the bars and maybe punch a few blocks loose to widen the hole, and moments later, a certain *boyar* was strangling people before they could make a peep.

Forget escaping via a window. What else did he have to work with?

At least they'd not stuck him in an oubliette, a fancy French word for hole in the ground. Those usually proved the hardest to escape from.

The floor, while dusty, proved clear. No grate covering a drain so they could sluice away blood and other fluids. Poor thinking if you asked him. The cement pad was free of debris. No bones of previous occupants—which weren't for eating, or so his mother said when she slapped them out of his hands at a young age. "No eating the leftovers," she told him. "The flesh and bones of our enemy taste best fresh."

Ah, the sweet lessons of youth. How he couldn't wait to pass on these nuggets of wisdom to his own cubs, cubs he planned to have with Teena, and they would hopefully inherit her perfect demeanor and patience. Golden-haired children with her sweet smile and what about those sparkling eyes?

Screech. Put on the brakes and slow down, tiger.

The drugs must still have him in their grip. Waxing poetic about a woman. Suffice it to say he liked her, liked her enough that he imagined a future with her. Hips or no hips. Funny how he did not give a damn about the width of them. He was obsessed with his wife, and her genes had nothing to do with it.

In Teena, he'd found someone he could converse with. Someone who listened to him and didn't belittle him, at least not in a cruel way. She could hold her own with her quick wit and melt him with a smile. She was kind, much kinder than him, but at the same time, she didn't cringe at the roughness life could dish out.

As to her habit of inspiring tiny mishaps—and not so tiny ones—he loved it. Life with his kitten would never be boring.

A tiger needed some excitement in his life.

A life that someone seemed determined to shorten.

No dying allowed. I don't care what the humans plan. It doesn't matter. Only one thing did. Getting out of here and back to his virgin wife. *So I can debauch her properly, bed or no bed.* This had gone on too long.

He kept studying his space. No cot to tear apart so he could steal the springs. Forget a frame he could use to chisel at rock or pry at the door.

The door didn't sport any hinges he could remove. Nor did it sport a lock he could pick. The metal portal to his prison proved impervious to his fist, and the thick steel frame, embedded in the rock, held only a tiny window, a wee square with bars only wide enough to wiggle fingers through.

Utterly useless for escaping, but it was a window to the outside.

After a quick sniff to ensure no one lurked outside the door—he'd learned that lesson when his family visited his uncle's dungeon up north and his sister bit him—he pressed close to the opening, searching for clues.

Nothing jumped out initially, but he did find himself admiring the ambiance.

Total dungeon vibe.

How he enjoyed the classics. In this case, an old dungeon that retained most of the fun characteristics that rendered it spooky, such as cobwebs in the corners—fat spiders being an awesome bonus, especially the hairy ones, which his sister hated, especially when tucked into her bed.

Totally worth the week of mucking out the stables that his mother made him do after.

The prison kept its medieval appeal with rock walls, cold, damp air, the faint rattle of chains. But it also incorporated smart modern conveniences like wrought-iron lights sculpted to appear like torches, the yellow glass cut in the shape of flame. Real torches were really awful, smoky and constantly in need of replacing. It could prove dangerous to hair as well if you walked too close and were in a stylish, long-and-shaggy phase.

The smell of burning hair to this day haunted him, especially when his sister left audio clips of his manly shouts of surprise on his voicemail.

No fire here. However, this dungeon had a solid freaking door that wouldn't budge no matter how hard he kicked it. Not even a dent.

It was enough to make his tiger flop into a heap of shame.

"Stop that. We are not a superhero with inconsistent great strength. This is one of those times when we must use our wits."

Of course his wits would work better if given some kind of tool. Since the only tool he had was his brain, he did the best thing he could for it. He took a nap.

Despite his slumber, when an outside noise was detected—furry swipe to his sleeping mind along with a tigerish version of *"Wake up, idiot."*—he sprang to wakefulness.

Someone approaches. Several someones judging by the irregular rhythm of thumping feet.

Finally some action.

Dmitri set the stage for confrontation. He sat and leaned against the back wall, an indolent pose with one leg straight, the other slightly bent, enough he could lean on it and adopt an expression of boredom. Also known as his *knyaz* look. Or, as Sasha named it, his haughty dick face.

And no, she didn't mean hottie. She'd laughed when he'd asked.

It should be noted that felines were especially noted for their indolent, casual poses. But never doubt they were ready to act within a blink of an eye.

The footsteps approached, and his tiger practically rolled in his mind with excitement.

Calm down. I need to figure out the situation first.

Then we play?

We will play hard, he assured.

The footsteps staggered to a halt, and close too. He could see the close shave on the head of the guy standing right before his tiny window. However, while his enemy hovered close, the opening in the door was too small and too far from him currently for him to catch any scents.

The scraping of metal and then the click of a tumbler turning. A lock was disengaged, and the squeak of a door in need of oil meant a door opened.

It just wasn't his door.

"Get in."

Aha, the familiar voice of the pilot who'd jumped.

I see I am in the right place for answers.

And after answers, *Playtime!* His tiger practically roared.

"Before I do, um, can you tell me if you've got another prisoner?"

"Maybe. We catch a lot of things out here."

"He's pretty noticeable. He's a tall guy and wide. Muscled and Russian. Did I mention very handsome? He's got a sexy smile and the most captivating blue eyes."

That voice. No. It couldn't be. Forgot nonchalance. Dmitri sprang to his feet and approached the bars in the door.

He didn't need to scent the sweet aroma to know Teena was in the hall outside his cell.

They've got my woman. My little kitten.

She'd gotten caught, and now they thought to toss his delicate wife in a cell. Unacceptable, and he'd do something to rectify it in a moment. It seemed she had company that didn't mind talking.

"Who is he to you?"

"My husband. We're newlyweds."

"Your husband?" The disparaging sneer came through loud and clear. "Animals don't marry. They rut. And fuck. In your case, your kind makes more monsters to infect our world."

"What do you mean my kind? Aren't we all human here?"

"Not all of us. Don't try and hide what you are. I know. I've been watching. Guarding against your infectious spread."

"Infectious? We're not a disease."

"No. You're worse. You're an abomination. To think you and others of your dirty kind have been living under our noses all this time."

"Dirty? I'll have you know we shower. With soap, I might add."

Dmitri could have laughed at her indignant reply, and yet at the same time, he could have shaken her. Antagonizing the human male with the obvious bias could get her hurt.

He lays a finger on her and he will die screaming.
Kill him anyway.

His tiger came up with the most brilliant suggestions.

"Such a smart mouth. It won't be so smart after I'm done with you. Did you know there's a market for women of your kind? Even oversized ones such as yourself."

Oversized? Had that man truly insulted his wife?

Rage built, simmering beneath his skin.

"You won't get away with this."

"I already have. No one knows where you are. Or even who holds you. And in a few days, weeks at the most, there will be no evidence left behind. Your tiger lover will be hunted and bagged, his fur kept as a trophy. As for you, maybe you'll last longer than the other women. You are, after all, made of sturdier stock. But the places I sell your kind to cater to a rough crowd. As you'll soon discover."

"My husband will kill you for that."

Such faith in him. Dammit. Even more pressure. This woman seemed determined to constantly challenge him.

His to-do list kept lengthening.

Save her from a dire situation— working on it.

Find a bed and debauch her properly—as soon as they got out of these cells.

Make her believe she was the one and only for him, the right one—he still had his work cut out for him there.

The noisy clump of half a dozen feet leaving saw him prowling and pacing the length of his cell. He waited until even the echo of their passage faded before springing to the door and peeking through.

Beautiful amber eyes met his via the window in the door across the hall. "Hello, husband. I have to say this honeymoon is really shaping up to be memorable. I don't think I've ever been held prisoner in a medieval prison before."

"Only the best for my little kitten." She laughed softly. He had to ask. "You are well? They did not injure you?"

"I am fine. Once I found them, I went with them willingly, hoping they'd put me close to you."

He frowned. "I don't understand. You intentionally went looking for the enemy?"

"Yes!" She beamed. "For once, I'm doing something completely crazy. My family will be so proud when they find out I got caught on purpose so I could rescue you."

"You did what!" He might have roared.

She didn't seem impressed. "Don't act so shocked. How else was I supposed to find you?"

"I was preparing to escape. You should have stayed where I left you." Completely irrational, but he didn't know what else to say. It both warmed him to the toes and appalled him that she cared enough to put herself in danger.

"I couldn't stay where you left me, which I might add was in a snow bank due to your driving skills."

"My skills are excellent."

"Says the man who lost his passenger. And then got caught."

Hold on. Did she roll her eyes at him? "I was drugged."

"And how did you like it?" A sassy retort.

He gave her the look that never worked on his sister but did wonders with his mother. "Would a set of diamond earrings say I'm sorry?"

"Depends on if it matches the wedding ring I

don't yet have and the necklace."

He blinked. Then smiled. "Done."

"By the way, I met your sister."

Her announcement totally derailed his train of thought—which involved her wearing glittering stones and gold, and nothing else.

"How the hell did you meet Sasha?"

"She was the one who found me when you dumped me in that snowbank. Together, we went looking for you, but you were gone, and then your mother—"

"You met my mother, too?"

"Yes. Delightful woman. I'm sure. Maybe she'll even like me once I can convince her I'm good enough for you."

"That will never happen." No one would ever be good enough for his mother's son.

"Then she and my dad will have something to talk about, as he'll never accept you. But let's ignore them for the moment. You wanted to know why I came to rescue you."

"Obviously you were seeking punishment. You do know if you wanted a spanking, you just had to ask."

Her turn to blink at him and moisten her lips with the tip of her pink tongue. "I must say, that sounds intriguing. But you're distracting me."

"Distraction is better than planning the demise of my mother and sister for allowing you to put yourself in harm's way."

"They didn't have a choice. I insisted when I found out it would take hours for the satellite to locate you. Then, in a weird stroke of luck, the dogs came back, so I got on the sled and told them to go home—"

"The dogs." He spoke the words faintly as he tried to wrap his head around the impossible series of events.

"Yes, those dogs we found. You know the ones who took a shine to me and that you drove off with after you dumped me in the snow."

He'd better add a bracelet to his jewelry shopping list. "They found you?"

"Yup. Anyhow, they took off with me in the sled, and you'll be proud to know I only fell off a few times before I got the hang of it. The puppies—"

Only she would call huskies, which could band together and tear even a tiger apart, puppies.

"—were nice enough to stop so I could get back on. Turns out, they knew the way back to their stable. I found this place, and eventually I ran into some guards who took me prisoner. And well"—she smiled, wide and beautiful—"here I am!"

Yes, she was here, but what of her cohorts? "One thing I do not understand is, if you intentionally set out to find me, what happened to my sister and mother? Where are they?"

"Last I saw them, they were tracking me with some kind of close-range GPS device that I stashed in my pants. They're part of my rescue plan. They shouldn't be far behind. Soon you'll be free again."

He banged his head on the bars he gripped, muttering, "No. No. No. This cannot be happening. If they rescue me, I shall never hear the end of it. This is a disaster."

"I'm sure they won't tease you. I mean it's not your fault you got captured by humans. There were a lot of them. And they had guns."

Oh way to deepen his shame. "No. I will not have it." He spoke the words low. "I will save myself dammit!" he yelled.

"You know, Daddy usually makes the walls tremble when he's really mad."

Okay, so he needed to crank up the rage a little bit. Being compared to her father? And coming up short? Yeah, that fired the adrenaline up a notch. He felt the edge of the door, seeking a weakness.

Teena kept chatting. "You'll be glad to know I'm still a virgin. When the men talked about testing the merchandise, I told them I was saving myself for my husband."

"They talked about touching you?" Ooh, that made him boil.

"Talked yes, acted no. Once the head honcho guy heard I was a virgin, he said it would fetch a higher price."

The guy wanted to sell his woman? For sex?

Dmitri huffed and puffed. His eyes narrowed, and he stared at the wall in his way.

"Then...oh dear. Something just moved in the corner. Dear god. No. No. No!"

Teena began to scream. And scream. And scream. The terror high-pitched and unacceptable.

With a roar, Dmitri ran at the mortared stone wall, shoulder first, rage his shield, and his body the wrecking ball.

Crack. Crumble. *Hack*.

Stupid dust lifted as the old stonework shattered at the impact, and still Teena screamed, the sound fueling his protective instincts.

Forget looking for a key or picking the lock. He shoved at the wall of her cell. He didn't have the same momentum in the tight hall. He threw himself at it once. Twice.

The third time, stone shifted—the ancient

masonry an easier task to break than solid steel— and he stumbled over the uneven debris right into Teena's cell.

"Where is it? Where is the monster?" Surely something horrendous threatened her.

Wide-eyed and backed against the wall, Teena gaped at him, alone and unhurt.

"Did you just bulldoze a wall?" she asked.

"Yes." He frowned. "You were just screaming. Why were you screaming?"

"Spider."

His turn to blink at her stupidly. "Spider? I don't understand."

"There was a big one. In here. With me."

"You were screaming because of a spider?"

"Well, yeah. It was big. And hairy," she confided with a shudder. "But you killed it when you came crashing through the wall. A big rock fell on it. My hero."

Some men might have stalked away in disgust. Others would have mocked her for her fear. Dmitri on the other hand? He beamed.

She called him her hero. He'd kill a spider every day if she kept thinking that way.

"Come, little kitten. Let us escape from this dungeon," he said with a flourish of his hands.

"Why not just wait for reinforcements?"

Wait for help? "Never." With that exclamation, he swept her into his arms, whirled back to the opening he'd made and realized they both wouldn't fit. He set her down, and once they'd both squeezed through, he swept her back into his arms.

A giggle burst from her. "Dmitri, what are you doing? I can walk."

"I am rescuing you, the proper way. The—"

"Russian way." She laughed. "Very well. Let's go."

Their going wasn't exactly stealthy. The halls truly were narrow, and two of the glass sconces covering the wall lights ended up shattering on the floor, yet the loud noise didn't draw guards.

A shame. This narrow space would have proven perfect to take them on one or two at a time.

Apparently the humans knew this would work against them, hence why Dmitri faced a sea of pointed guns, when he opened the door at the top of the stairs leading into the main part of the keep.

Facing imminent doom, a tiger could perhaps regret his hasty decision to execute his own escape instead of waiting for his sister and other backup.

Nah. He'd never go down without a fight. Except now, he didn't have just himself to think of.

Still nestled in his arms, Teena buried her face against his neck. The poor thing was probably terrified. He had to strain to hear her whispered, "Throw me."

"What?" He practically barked the word, and a half-dozen weapons bobbled as sweaty fingers clutched at triggers.

"Throw me at them," she hissed in a low tone. "I'll take the three in the middle, you get the rest."

It was only as he felt her body beginning to shift in his grip that he understood; she was going wild.

Here comes my lioness.

Some people thought the male lions were king, but when it came to hunting, it was the females you had to watch for.

Trusting his kitten, he tossed her. And, no, the irony wasn't lost on him that instead of the human getting thrown to the lions, it was the lion getting thrown at the humans.

And the tiger going after the rest.

Shapeshifting in some respects felt as if it took a lot of time, but in reality, once the magic that manipulated their cell structure was called upon, the actual time of change was little. Little enough that, when his lunge ended, he was already swiping with claw-tipped paws.

Men screamed. A few guns did go off, resulting in more screams. Not from him or his wife. Guns proved effective only if well aimed.

The smell of panic mixed and swirled with that of fresh blood and aconite. How he loved the smell of battle. What he liked less were the shreds of his shirt that still clung to him.

Nothing worse than looking like an idiot who couldn't shift right. But at least his mishap wasn't as bad as Teena's, who still wore her thong.

In mere moments, the room had only two felines standing. Bodies littered the floor, some groaning, most not. The faint yells of a couple that fled sifted back to them.

His golden lioness flicked her tail and peered at the door.

He dipped his own head and swept a paw, gesturing, "After you."

On second thought, he didn't want her to face possible harm. He'd go first.

He slapped down her tail and pinned it. Over her shoulder she shot him an amber-eyed glare and a growl.

Releasing her tail, he swatted her furry butt then trotted past her.

Whack.

She swatted his ass.

He flicked his tail in acknowledgement of her

compliment. Of course she admired his fine form, even when he wore his tiger, his butt was awesome.

Taking the lead, he went into stealth mode. Crouched low, he slunk along the wide hall. Smells surrounded him, mostly mundane ones like the floor wax used on the gleaming wooden floors and the faint delicious aroma of bacon frying. Had they missed breakfast?

Forget food made by hands. He was after a different meal today, and lucky him, there was the cologne he looked for.

Intent on his trail, he almost missed the slight creak of a door opening behind him.

As he whirled his head and spotted the man with the gun, he noted Teena, not looking in front of her, nose to the ground, barreling into his legs. With a yell, the fellow toppled, the gun went off, and the bullet ricocheted, back to its sender.

Teena let out a loud breath and gave the lion equivalent of a shrug.

And she calls that bad luck.

Hardly.

Adopting his awesome slink once again, Dmitri stalked the scent trail of the man wearing the spicy cologne.

He found him, standing by a massive floor-to-ceiling fireplace, an inefficient monstrosity. Yet, for all its impractical nature, considering the amount of wood required to feed it, not to mention the sooty nature of wood smoke, those flaws enhanced the beauty and framed the intimidation factor. *Look at me. I'm so rich I can burn a shit-ton of money and still freeze my human ass off in this room.*

His tiger summed it more succinctly.

Idiot. Let's eat him.

Enemy. Check.

Fresh. Check.

Hungry? *Very.* And the idiot in front of him was making him wait to sate his *hunger.*

"Stop right there, or else." The human with the spicy scent aimed his double-barrel shotgun at Dmitri.

One gun? Bad odds—for the guy holding it. Especially since the human appeared in the mood to chat. Villains were predictably dumb that way. The more in control they felt, the less they pulled the trigger.

Dmitri would know. He enjoyed a good gloat when he'd pulled one over on an enemy. Watching their faces as he espoused on a lovely strangulation, the blanching of their eyes as he poured cement on their feet. Good times.

If he was in a playful mood and looking to update the sound effect he used for text messages, then he sometimes resorted to a sneak and pounce, ensuring beforehand he had his sister following with a cell phone to record. Sasha did a great job after of splicing the audio file so that his minions visibly shuddered when his phone went off.

How I love being me.

Swapping from tiger to man took but a moment, and he stretched, his dewy, human skin shivering in the brisk air of the room. "If it's not the lunch that got away. So nice of you to come to me," Dmitri said.

"I didn't come to you. I captured you."

"If you say so." Dmitri shrugged and beamed his most placating smile. Since Sasha wasn't here to plant her fist in it, he felt rather safe using it.

The pompous human glared. "Stop trying to be clever. Just because you're using words and put on a human face doesn't change anything, beast."

"My name is Dmitri, although that is reserved for friends and family. You, you may call me *knyaz*. My prince works too."

"You have no name. No title. All you are to me is a trophy." The human waved his hand in a wide sweep that encompassed the mounted heads on the walls. Faces frozen in a rictus, marbled eyes catching the lamplight, the taxidermied heads played silent witness to their discussion.

"You killed all of these animals." Dmitri stated, didn't ask.

The man sneered. "Every single one. Dirty beast people. And pathetic to boot. I expected more sport from your kind. I even gave them all a fair chance to run. Not my fault the hunter was mightier than they were."

The human bragged about his murders. And for what? Sport?

I'll show him who is master of the sport. Dmitri also enjoyed hunting, especially those who killed his kin—such as poor stuffed Jorge in the corner, who just wanted to putter in his garden. No more fresh tomatoes from the vine. Mother would not be pleased.

Fear not, Jorge, I will avenge you. And avenge all the others who had perished at this idiot's hands.

First, though, the legalities, because killing humans for fun was prohibited. Bloody spoilsports in charge. "Wife, please note, should you be asked later by the tribunal, that this human does hereby admit his guilt in the blatant pursuit and murder of kindred spirits. It is my belief that these are hate crimes. The human shows a disturbing disregard for what he's done and general…" Dmitri paused, looking for a word.

Teena supplied it, having also shifted, and

praise be, that damn thong was at least covering part of her. "Idiocy."

"What?" He'd forgotten what they were talking about.

"I said the human hunter is an idiot. Which means there's only one verdict."

"Guilty. He must die."

Click. A throat cleared. "Excuse me, but you both seem to have forgotten I'm the one holding the fucking gun."

"Oh dear. That really probably wasn't a good idea," Teena muttered before she lunged at the hunter.

And that was when her mighty power, which he was going to start calling "making-shit-happen" kicked in.

Rawr.

Chapter Twenty-two

Diving toward the guy holding the gun, Teena could only hope that her usual ill luck would strike.

Or was Dmitri right? Did she perhaps just have a different type of luck?

As she soared through the air, very conscious that her unfettered breasts led the way, she just hoped she could startle the human with the gun enough to get the upper edge.

She startled him all right.

Only the whites of his eyes showed, and his jaw dropped as he staggered back from her, changing the trajectory of his aim. He recovered enough to pull the trigger, but that type of gun had a huge recoil. The gun bucked, the barrel swung, and apparently she had a lot in common with a barn. She was impossible to miss.

Ow.

He shot me.

Just the graze of a bullet, though, enough to nick skin and make her bleed.

He might as well have waved a red flag in front of her husband.

Apparently, it wasn't just tigers who could leap a dozen feet in a single bound. Her husband coiled those muscled thighs of his and soared through the air to land on the hunter.

As he rapped the head of the human on the floor, he growled. "You." *Bang.* "Don't." *Whack.* "Shoot." *Bop.* "My wife." A rapid set of taps. "Bad human. Dead human. Judgment carried."

With a final crack, the cause for their troubles stared sightlessly at a ceiling, where a massive eagle floated on fishing line.

The cognizant part of Teena found the violence off-putting, but the predator in her—and face it, she was more hunter than prey—-liked that her mate had taken care of the threat.

"Good kitty." She purred the words.

He heard. The massive body turned, still in a crouch. With a growly noise, he dropped their dead enemy, but danger still radiated from his skin, a vibrating tenseness that truly was sexy.

Look at that naked skin. So close and begging for a lick.

How about a rub even? Was it something in her expression, the fact that her nipples hardened, or did he feel the same thing? She didn't know or really care.

They didn't need an excuse to come together in a clash of bodies. Their arms wound around the other, their lips meshed with passion and breathlessness.

"We have got to stop meeting this way," he said.

"How? Do you mean going from one calamity to another? Get used to it. This is what happens around me. We have to take our moments when and where we can." She nipped at his neck.

She couldn't miss the shudder that went through him.

"Wrap your legs around my waist."

She did as told but still asked, "Why?"

"We are not going anywhere until I claim you."

"Um, Dmitri, I hate to point out the obvious, but we're going somewhere, and, guess what, still unclaimed over here."

"Don't confuse me with details, little kitten. I am too aroused to think straight. We are finding a spot that I might give you the wedding night we skipped."

"What's wrong with right here?" she asked as Dmitri jogged through a kitchen with lovely gleaming counters, and an older woman rolling dough. Or at least frozen in the action of, pin held over the floury ball, her jaw hanging.

"Hello there, cook. I am going to debauch my wife, which shall leave me famished. I'll double your salary if have a good-sized breakfast for me and my kitten in about an hour."

"An hour?" Tina squeaked.

"You're right. That's too long. Given the level of my need for you, more like fifteen minutes. But I can wait at least thirty minutes for food. We can cuddle while we wait."

"Dmitri. That is so…so…"

"Russian?" he supplied with a grin.

She laughed. "Perfect!"

Dmitri proved his single-mindedness in hunting them down a bedroom. Two flights of stairs? He wasn't even breathing hard at the top. Did he panic or grouse when the enemy stepped into view holding a knife? Nope, he just dodged sideways. The thug lunged, tripped on his untied bootlace—talk about ill luck— and tumbled down the stairs. She winced when she saw where the knife landed.

Dmitri whooped. "Look at that, kitten. You're like kryptonite to my enemy."

"You're quoting superhero comic book stuff now? What happened to romance novels?"

"Superheroes always get the girl." He winked as he swung open a door and then kicked it shut with a foot.

"Are we there yet?" she teased.

"We are. I present to you, a bed." Over to the massive frame he strode, and with a smile, he dropped her on the mattress.

She hit the springs. They contracted then, with an almost audible *boing*, expanded, sending her up, which might not have been too bad except Dmitri lunged to grab her, hit the side of the bed, and toppled. He didn't squish her, just landed on the mattress, but a puny made-for-human bed was no match for a tiger and a lioness.

Crack. Thump. The bed collapsed on one side, and Teena bounced again, this time right off it.

This had happened enough times that she knew to tuck, roll, and then sprawl on the thick fur covering the floor—sniff, the mundane kind thank goodness.

"Kitten! Get back on this bed this instance."

She rolled her head to see Dmitri had rolled onto his back on the sadly listing bed. Given it still had three more legs that could collapse, she stayed where it was safe.

But lonely.

She patted the spot beside her. "Oh. Dmitri."

"No. There is a perfectly fine bed right here."

Crack.

Another leg cracked at the head, and the tilt changed the angle and rolled Dmitri. He didn't wait to see where he'd land. To his feet he sprang, towering over her.

Six foot plus of prime male flesh. Naked male flesh. *Mine.*

Oh yes.

Did her gaze give her away? Perhaps it was the lick of her lips that made his eyes smolder. Whatever the reason, in a blink, he was by her side, kneeling on the rug, his lips seeking out hers. Their mouths clung together, oblivious to where they were. Only one thing mattered.

We have to touch.

It wasn't an option anymore; it was a necessity. The need burned within. The compelling urge to have him come within her, to claim her—and claim him—overrode all other concerns.

It seemed the same urgency possessed him. His mouth might be content to sip and taste from hers, but his hands were on a mission of exploration.

Callused fingertips rubbed the soft skin of her belly, sliding over her skin, eager to touch and taste. Taste skin that hadn't seen a shower in a while.

"Hold on," she said. As she rolled away to her side, breaking the embrace, she propelled her self to her feet.

He might have uttered, "Get back here. I was not done," but she ignored him. Just like he ignored his own command, staggering to his feet with a growled, "Kitten."

Did it have to do with the fact that she stripped as she sashayed away? As to her destination, a bedroom in a place like this had exactly what she needed, a bathroom and, even better, a large walk-in shower.

For her first time, she'd like to at least be bathed. Clean for the dirty acts to come.

Naked, and unabashed, she stood for a moment and basked in the heat of his smoldering gaze. The skin between her shoulders prickled, her skin hyper aware.

She couldn't resist and peeked over her shoulder. In sucked her breath.

He's magnificent.

Dark hair tousled by their play. The haughty lines of his face stark with need.

A need for her.

She stepped into the shower and gasped as she turned the knob, the cold water spritzing her but quickly getting warm.

His nostrils flared, yet he said not a word. He didn't need to. Erotic tension poured off him, his entire body held taut and coiled, ready to spring.

So dangerous.

So hot.

Mine

"Come here," she demanded. Who was this bold Teena? This brazen temptress who called to him?

Did he hear her thoughts? Because he answered. "You are mine."

Possession could be a sexy thing.

He came to her, her husband and soon-to-be lover. The large shower quickly became cramped.

It was perfect. His body brushed against hers, igniting all her nerve endings. His hands took to rubbing circuitously over her back, each time widening the circle of his stroke. He built the tension, moving closer and closer to...

"Aaah." Her head went back as she sighed. His hands cupped the swell of her breasts, weighing them in his big palms. The slight squeeze created small shivers.

Against the cold tile wall of the shower, he pressed her, his big body cushioning against hers. A thigh split apart her own, the bunched muscle a shuddering pleasure to grip and rub against.

Her sex reveled in the friction against his leg. But it wasn't what she ultimately wanted.

She reached down and grasped him, the thick root of his cock barely fitting in her grip.

So wide. And the length... Up the slickness of

his shaft her hand slid, the hot steel, hard, rock hard actually, and almost alive. It tensed and pulsed as she played with it. For every sign of pleasure, a quiver went through her sex.

Now. Please now.

She must have whispered it aloud because he answered. "Yes. But not here."

He stepped from the shower, and she could have sobbed at the loss of contact. But he quickly drew her after him, wrapping her in a fluffy towel before sweeping her into his arms and stepping into the bedroom. The bed still leaned at an angle.

He looked so pained. Poor guy with his obsession on making her first time perfect.

"I know you've got your heart set on a bed, but don't a lot of romances say a rug in front of a fireplace is just as good?"

Lucky for them it was a gas fireplace because Dmitri set her on the plush carpet and insisted on lighting it for effect.

She might have complained, except it gave her a moment to calm down and to admire the movement of his ass when he hunted for the dial to activate the gas-burning hearth.

Flickering flames danced behind him as he spun with a pleased look. Back to her side he came, leaning down and resuming their kiss and the press of their bodies.

Had she thought she'd cooled down during that respite? Never. The banked fire flared to life, even more intense than before. The throb of her sex demanded satisfaction.

She threaded her fingers through his hair, holding him close to her as her hips angled below him.

A sharp nip of his lower lip had him chuckling.

"Are you ready for me, kitten?"

Would he stop torturing her? She bit the column of his throat, a firm chomp, hard enough to break a little skin, enough to give her a more primal taste of her man.

He let out a sound, unlike any, a cross between a roar and a groan.

The teasing ended.

The head of his wide shaft nudged at her lips. It dipped into the dewing honey, wetting itself. As his lips claimed hers, fierce and controlling, he pushed.

Oh my.

It was unlike anything she'd imagined, the stretch so noticeable, and yet...pleasurable. He might prove a snug fit, but it was happening.

She dug her nails into his back, arching at his slow penetration that turned into a sharp tug of pain.

He'd breached her maidenhead.

...and kept going.

Her breath came in hiccupping pants, her whole body tense and coiled. His hips were rotating against her, grinding himself into her. It was fucking incredible.

Her mouth opened in a soundless scream. She arched. She clung to him and, at the same, time pushed away.

The intensity. The pleasure... The—

Like a slow wave, a big one, followed by more soldier waves, ranks and ranks of them, rolled through her body.

She might have called his name. She might have possibly died.

But one thing was for sure.

He's mine.

Chapter Twenty-three

She is mine.

A primitive thought to have but appropriate given he nipped the lobe of her ear. Some liked to mark the skin of the neck or upper shoulder. But Dmitri was quite fond of those sensitive little ears.

So he claimed one, used it to place his mark.

There was something about the act, or maybe it was the knowledge behind it that made it more potent. He was now married in all ways to this woman.

They would spend a lifetime together.

"What are you thinking?" she asked when her breathing slowed.

He caught her amber gaze and smiled. "Just thinking that you're perfect."

"Fire."

"Yes, hot too."

"No, I really mean fire. Like behind you."

Indeed, during their somewhat strenuous activities, the rug had shifted and bunched against the open fireplace. Flames licked along the fur.

Poor Teena looked appalled. "I'm sorry. I should have known better than to let you light fire around me.

But Dmitri didn't curse or panic. He laughed as he jumped to his feet and dumped a nearby vase of flowers on the rug. "No worries. It's out." He turned and wagged a finger at her. "Don't you dare apologize, kitten. Personally, I think your skill will be a great asset."

"How do you figure?"

"I predict the construction economy will boom, and I already own a good chunk of it. I see us attending many dinner parties and social gatherings."

"Dmitri!" Before she could say anything else— although judging by the mirth in her eyes, most of her shock was feigned—the door to the room was kicked open.

Even as the door bounced off the wall, Dmitri was moving. With one hand, he snagged the cover on the bed, whirled it over Teena, and then crouched in a ready position in front of her.

He then groaned as his new father-in-law yelled, "Never fear, baby girl. Daddy is here!" And while the other man aimed a gun, he'd not yet fired it.

What do you know, I think my new father-in-law likes me. Unlike his daughter at the moment.

"Daddy, go away!" she squeaked, her cheeks crimson bright and the blanket he'd given her pulled up to her chin.

"But I'm here to um...save you?" Peter looked from Dmitri, who smiled and shrugged, to his daughter on the floor, who glared. "Fuck me, don't tell me you mated the damned Russian."

"I did, and will you stop calling him that?"

"Or else?"

"Don't make me sic Mommy on you."

Peter shuddered. "Now that's just plain evil, baby girl."

"Who's evil?" Sasha asked as she sauntered in the room. She let out an unladylike whistle as she took in the broken bed, the smoldering end of the rug, and his blushing bride on the floor—who couldn't get any redder if she tried.

No wait. He was wrong. That was surely a brand-new shade of crimson never before seen.

"Where is my son? What has that *human* done to him?"

He could totally understand his kitten's mortification. Was it unmanly to admit he also wanted to crawl under the blanket with his bride?

But hey, at least he'd made her first time memorable.

And not long after, he gave her a wedding to remember—that didn't require drugs! He even invited her family. To think, they called him crazy. After meeting some of her relatives, he begged to differ.

The day they wed for a second time proved beautiful. The bride wore white despite his mother's insistence she shouldn't, given they'd been caught in flagrante delicto. But in this, Teena's mother got her way. No one ever quite knew what happened behind closed doors, but the thumping and the not so neatly coiffed hair when the two matriarchs exited caused more than a few speculations.

Despite the priest tripping on the hem of his hassock and crushing the flowers, the organist having broken a hand and playing only deep chords, as well as the caterer getting ill at the last moment and them ordering in massive amounts of fast food, the day was perfect.

Teena was perfect.

She's mine.

A tiger's bride, and as he whispered, later on that night as he held her in his arms, her skin dewed with pleasure, in a bed, FINALLY, "Always know I choose you."

And even more awesome, she chose him right

back.

"You are mine." Words they both liked to shout during the throes of passion.

Epilogue

About nine months later, and yes, Dmitri's mother counted.

Don't yell. It's not manly.

Dmitri managed to restrain himself, but barely. His wife had a killer grip, especially when in pain, but he could bear it to help her, even if he might never grip a pen again. He held his wife's hand and managed not to wince even when she crushed it tight. A light perspiration dotted her brow, and she panted as the contractions hit.

He murmured supportive words. He'd learned his lesson. Dmitri had questioned only once how women could tolerate the pain of change so well and yet lamented the labor of childbirth. Grandma, who'd birthed thirteen cubs, taught him a valuable lesson that day.

As his wife labored, he was reminded of the fact that he'd debated being present for the birth of his child. His mother thought it unseemly for a lord to be present during woman's work. His grandmother was aghast. His sister, however, mocked him.

"Pussy," she'd sneered when he'd elucidated his reasons for remaining out of the birthing room.

What male could stand to have his manhood questioned? When the midwife arrived, Dmitri remained in the bedroom, standing at the head of the bed, both anticipating the arrival of his child and horrified at the pain he put his poor kitten through.

"We should have gone to a hospital where you could have had drugs for the pain," he said as yet another wave shuddered through his Teena's body.

"No drugs," she gasped. "This. Is. Perfectly. Natural!" she shouted as yet another contraction gripped her.

Natural? Dmitri wasn't sure he agreed but too late for second thoughts now. The baby was coming. His son. His mini-me. The male who would carry on his name and dynasty.

Or so he assumed. The ultrasound never was able to clearly indicate the sex due to the placement of the placenta, and Teena refused any further testing, claiming she wanted it to be a surprise.

Surprise. There was a word that kind of described life now. Every day was a new adventure with his wife. His speed and agility had become quite honed as he dove, dodged, and fought back the forces of trouble that plagued his wife.

Now that she had a hero in her corner, even she admitted to Dmitri that maybe her power wasn't so bad. Mostly because they had each other. And soon, their son.

With much gore, screaming—some by him— his child burst forth into the world with a mighty wail.

A touch lightheaded, Dmitri sat down hard on the stool by his wife's head, still clasping her hand. He blinked as the baby, his child, had its cord cut and clipped and a blanket whirled around it.

The midwife held out the bundle to him. "Your daughter, milord."

A daughter? But he'd ordered a son. The midwife, though, didn't care. She handed him the yelling baby. So light. He barely noted the weight of her in his arms. He glanced at her, noting only her little face peeked from the fabric.

Their gazes locked. The crying halted.

Giant blue eyes blinked at him, framed in thick lashes. A little rosebud of a mouth pursed, then curled into a smile—which no amount of argument later would sway him was caused by gas.

His heart constricted, and his breath caught. *This is my daughter.*

My child. My daughter.

Good lord. With his genes and her mother's, she would be perfect. Beyond perfect. Stupendous. And boys would eventually notice her fabulousness, which would mean…

As all the various realizations crashed into him, he hugged his daughter to him tight, even as he made plans to get a bigger castle. One with a moat. Filled with gators.

Oh and guard towers. Manned with guns.

And…

"That's not placenta. There's another baby coming!" the midwife exclaimed, breaking his inner epiphany.

Another?

Indeed. Within minutes, Dmitri held two absolutely perfect daughters.

"I hope you're not disappointed. I know you wanted a son," Teena said as she held out her arms for a bundle.

As he nestled a child in the crook of his wife's arms that she might cuddle and see the wonderful children she'd created, he couldn't help but smile.

"Disappointed? Never. My little czarinas shall dazzle everyone with their beauty. Rule the world with their greatness." As he expounded on the many virtues their children would surely possess, his wife smiled and mouthed, 'I love you'.

And the great thing was, "I love you, too, little kitten." Now and always.

The End

Author's Note: I truly hope you enjoyed this story. While this is the end of this series (at least for now), I have many other shapeshifter tales that might intrigue you. Visit my website for a full list at EveLanglais.com

You can also *stalk* me in the following places:
Facebook: bit.ly/faceevel
Twitter: @evelanglais
Goodreads: bit.ly/evelgood
Newsletter: Evelanglais.com/newrelease